WOLF
BLO

D0121239

WOLF BLOOD

Wolves Among Us

SHARON GOSLING

Piccadilly
PRESS

For Molly, and Beatrice

First published in Great Britain in 2015 by
PICCADILLY PRESS
80–81 Wimpole St, London W1G 9RE
www.piccadillypress.co.uk

Based on the series created by Debbie Moon

A CIP catalogue record for this book is available
from the British Library.

ISBN: 978-1-84812-519-3
also available as an ebook

1
Typeset by Palimpsest Book Production Ltd, Falkirk, Stirlingshire

Printed and bound by Clays Ltd, St Ives Plc

FSC

Piccadilly Press supports the Forest Stewardship Council (FSC),
the leading international forest certification organisation, and is
committed to printing only on Greenpeace-approved
FSC-certified paper.

Piccadilly Press is an imprint of Bonnier Publishing Fiction,
a Bonnier Publishing company
www.bonnierpublishingfiction.co.uk
www.bonnierpublishing.co.uk

One

The moon wasn't quite full yet, but it would be soon. Rhydian Morris looked up as it glinted in the clouded night sky. There was a time not long ago that he'd have been excited at the idea of wolfing out, but not any more. Not since Maddy Smith and her family had been forced to leave Stoneybridge. Now he'd have to wander the night alone, as if he was back to being a lone wolf. He'd finally found a pack, one that wanted him and that he wanted to be with, and then . . .

He felt something in his chest, a feeling too huge to fit into words.

He threw back his head and he *howled*.

Tom Okanawe and Shannon Kelly heard him. They were searching the Smiths' dark, abandoned house. Shannon had thought she'd seen lights driving up to it, but there was nothing there.

'Poor Rhydian,' she sighed, as the lonely sound of howling drifted to them again.

'It's all right for *him*,' said Tom, with a flash of annoyance, 'wolfing out on the moors.'

Shannon sighed. 'Tom, we all miss her. Come on. Let's go home.'

Shannon turned around and the light from her torch cut across the room. They both jumped out of their skins as a face stared back at them through the window. They rushed outside, but the woman had gone.

The thing about being in on the secret about Wolfbloods, Shannon thought next morning, was that everything else seemed pretty silly, really. Take, for example, the three Ks' latest scheme. Katrina's family had bought Bernie's place and had turned it into a diner where all three girls would work. They had even asked Shannon to sing on the opening night. Her boyfriend, Harry Averwood, was going to play guitar.

Boyfriend. Even thinking the word was weird. Anyway, there were other things to worry about. She and Tom waited for Rhydian and then bundled him into the photography club's darkroom to tell him what they had seen the previous night.

'It was definitely Doctor Whitewood,' said Tom.

'Why come back now?' Shannon wondered. The last time they had encountered the woman, she'd managed to get hold of some of Maddy's DNA. She was the reason the Smiths had fled Stoneybridge. That was two months ago.

'Well, she won't find any more DNA,' said Tom. 'We've scrubbed that house clean.'

'As long as she's only looking for the Smiths, you'll be safe,' Shannon told Rhydian, although he didn't seem to be listening at all.

'Shouldn't you be bouncing off the walls?' Tom asked. 'It being almost full moon, and all?'

Rhydian frowned. 'I'm fine,' he said, even though they all knew he wasn't.

'You've told Mrs Vaughan you're staying at Tom's tonight, right?' Shannon asked.

'Yeah,' Rhydian muttered, heading out of the door. Tom and Shannon followed.

'You'll need to be careful if Whitewood's on the prowl,' Shannon warned Rhydian. 'Just get as far away from Stoneybridge as you can.'

Rhydian still didn't seem to be listening. Mr Jefferies appeared, hustling everyone into the classroom. 'Come on, you lot! Hope you haven't forgotten what day it is?'

'Course not, sir,' said Katrina brightly. 'It's opening night! Drinks and live music from Shannon and Harry at the Kafe!'

'The . . . *Kafe*?' Jeffries repeated, pronouncing the name the same way Katrina had, as if it rhymed with 'safe'.

'With a K,' Katrina explained proudly. 'My idea.'

'Well, that's very creative, Katrina, but I was actually talking about the Careers Fair today. With a C.'

The Careers Fair was being held in the school hall. Rhydian really couldn't be bothered with any of it, and he wasn't the only one. Jimi Chen and Liam Hunter couldn't see the point either – Liam because he'd decided he'd be working on the farm with his dad and Jimi because he only wanted to work for himself.

'Working for anyone else is a chump's game,' he declared. 'I'll be a millionaire before I'm twenty-five.'

'Depressing thing is he probably will be,' Shannon muttered, as Rhydian opened the door to the hall.

Rhydian froze. There was another Wolfblood here. He could *smell* them.

'Rhydian?' Shannon asked. 'What is it?'

He didn't answer. Rhydian was completely focused on following the scent trail, snaking through the maze of desks and notice boards that had been set up in the hall. It led him to a smart arrangement of desks that was recruiting for a company involved in the big business of science and development. There were posters of people smiling at Petri dishes in meticulously clean laboratories, of engineers drilling wells in hot and dusty countries, of people sitting around conference tables.

SEGOLIA, said the sign.

WORKING TOGETHER FOR ALL OUR FUTURES, declared the company's slogan.

Rhydian stopped, watching the two people behind the desk. One was a young man wearing a suit. There was nothing interesting about him – not for Rhydian, at least. But the other . . .

She was Wolfblood, but not like any he'd ever seen before. The woman looked perfect – sharp suit, gleaming hair, neat nails. He couldn't imagine her wolfing out, running through the woods just for the sheer fun of it.

The woman was talking to Kara. Rhydian tuned into his Wolfblood hearing and heard her say, 'We're also the leading innovator in medical and genetic research.'

'It says here you can sponsor the most promising students through university,' Kara said, pointing at one of the company's prospectuses.

The woman was having trouble concentrating – she knew he was watching her, and she also knew he was Wolfblood. She sent Kara to talk to her human colleague and then turned to look at Rhydian.

'Hello, Rhydian,' she said, just loud enough for him to hear. 'Maddy says to say hi.'

Rhydian moved closer, picking up one of the Segolia brochures. The woman glanced around to make sure no one was watching and then moved to stand beside him.

'You know Maddy?'

'Yes. Her father called, said they were going into the wild. We offered them something better. My name's Dacia Turner – graduate recruiter for the Segolia Corporation. That's one of the things Segolia does. We've set up a new life for them in Canada. Once they're settled, she'll be in contact. This was an opportunity to let you know what's going on.'

Rhydian couldn't take it all in. 'Segolia? It's . . . run by Wolfbloods?'

Dacia shook her head. 'A few employees know the secret, though most don't. But some of our staff and several senior executives are Wolfbloods.'

Rhydian tried to imagine it, but he couldn't. 'Sat behind a desk all day . . .'

'It's not all paperwork. We protect and serve the company's interests. And our own.'

Rhydian almost laughed at that. 'What? Like a Segolia MI6?'

'If you like. Our interests are global. There's a lot of travel and the perks are great. At full moon they fly us out to Norway. In a private jet.'

'It's a bit smaller scale up here,' Rhydian told her.

'I'm looking forward to it.'

Rhydian gave her a look. 'What?'

'I've given up Norway to meet you. The least you can do is show me a full moon Stoneybridge style.'

'Not much "style" to it,' he said, quietly. 'Just me.'

Dacia smiled gently. 'That's the best thing about this job,' she said. 'Having a pack you belong to.'

Rhydian backed away and went to find Tom and Shannon, dragging them both outside to tell them what had happened. Shortly afterwards, he almost wished he hadn't. To say that Tom and Shannon were excited would be an understatement.

'Wolfblood Incorporated! That is so cool!' Tom crowed. 'Private jets, sharp suits . . . spying!' He tried to strike a cool James-Bond-style pose. 'The name's Okanawe,' he drawled. '*Tom* Okanawe.'

Shannon was just as bad. She immediately went into full-on daydream mode. 'They have a big science division? Imagine the research they must be doing! This is perfect for me!' She was on her back on one of the picnic benches in the playground, staring up at the sky. 'They probably know everything. Why exactly you are like you are. How it all works . . .' She sat up and looked at Rhydian. 'You will put in a good word for me, right? I have to work there, even if it's after university.' Shannon glanced across the playground and then jumped off the bench to hide. 'Oh no!'

Rhydian and Tom looked around, confused. Then Tom saw Harry.

'Shan,' he said. 'Are you hiding from your own boyfriend?'

Harry headed back into the school and Shannon got up. 'He wants to rehearse again,' she groaned. 'And we have bigger things going on today, right?'

Rhydian nodded. 'Yeah, actually, we have. Check it out.' He jerked his chin at the edge of the playground. Standing there, watching, was Dr Whitewood. He began to walk towards her, but Tom and Shan stopped him.

'Go inside,' Tom told him. 'You're not on her radar. We are.'

'I'll deal with her,' Shannon promised. She left Tom and Rhydian and marched right up to Whitewood. 'Doctor Whitewood. Shall I get Mr Jeffries?'

Whitewood looked Shannon up and down with a cold smile. 'Oh, I'm fine here. Call it scientific research.'

Shannon snorted. 'On what, football and gossip?'

The woman glared at her. 'I'm disappointed in you, Shannon. You say you want to be a scientist, yet here you are, concealing the truth. Denying the evidence.'

'You told everyone you'd found werewolves, but when it came to providing evidence, you couldn't get any,' said Shannon.

'Because you and your werewolf friends took it,' the doctor hissed. 'You could have cleared my name any time, and you chose not to. Why? Was it just to protect Maddy, or are you and your friend Tom werewolves too?'

Before Shannon could think of an answer, Mr Jeffries appeared.

'Doctor Whitewood,' he said. 'What a surprise. Let's take this elsewhere, shall we?'

Rhydian followed as the teacher led Whitewood to his office and shut the door. Then he listened to what was going on inside.

'You can't just walk into a school like this,' Jeffries told her.

Whitewood gave a harsh laugh. 'Oh no – I might lose my job! No, wait . . . I've already lost that, along with my friends and my reputation. Remind me, Tim, what exactly have I got to lose?'

Rhydian heard Jeffries sigh. 'Rebecca, you can't go on like this.'

'I had evidence,' Whitewood said, her voice flat and cold. 'It was stolen.'

'And I saw Maddy Smith with two pet timber wolves,' the teacher told her. 'No full moon. There was no magic or monsters.'

Whitewood made a frustrated sound. 'The bones we excavated didn't steal themselves! You were there! Those tunnels, Liam's video, the DNA – how much evidence do you need before you see a pattern? Or maybe you don't want to see it. Maybe you've got a reason not to?'

'Oh, for goodness' sake!' Jeffries snapped. 'Yeah –

you're right. I'm a werewolf!' He made a pathetic snarling sound, which didn't even sound like a dog, let alone a wolf. There was silence and then he said, 'I'm sorry. Rebecca, look –'

Rhydian jumped away from the door as Whitewood barrelled towards it, angry and hurt.

'I feel bad,' said Shannon, once Rhydian had told them what he'd heard. 'She's desperate.'

Rhydian was not impressed. 'You're sorry for *Whitewood*?'

'Look,' said Tom, before an argument could break out. 'Full moon is our chance to get rid of her. She thinks either we're werewolves, or that we'll lead her to some. But we'll be at the Kafe all evening.'

Shannon perked up. 'And if she doesn't see anything, she'll think Maddy's family were the only ones and leave us alone!'

'Exactly,' said Tom. 'Everything's going to be fine.'

Rhydian wasn't listening. He was looking at a text that said: MEET B4 MOONRISE ;) DACIA.

Two

The night was just tipping towards dusk when Rhydian and Dacia met up. They ran through the forest, side by side, their wolf selves set free even before they had transformed. Rhydian felt as if he could hear everything, see everything – every creature, every blade of grass, every leaf. He couldn't imagine ever wanting to be anywhere but right there.

'I don't understand how anyone can live in a city,' Rhydian told her. 'Cars, noise, people. We belong out here.'

'Not if you're alone,' she said.

Rhydian frowned. 'I'm not alone. Tom and Shan are my pack.'

Dacia shook her head. 'Not really. You can trust them all you like – stay friends forever. But they'll never be one of us.'

Rhydian turned to face her. 'What do you want me to do? I had a pack, a family. *You* sent them to Canada.'

He walked away, but Dacia didn't get the hint. She followed him.

'Did you ever meet your own parents?' she asked.

Rhydian shrugged. 'My mum. Even lived with her for a bit, but . . . living wild isn't exactly my thing.'

Dacia stopped. 'Whoa,' she said. 'Your mum's a *wild* Wolfblood?' When Rhydian nodded she shook her head in amazement. 'I've never met one. My dad died,' she added quietly. 'I was pretty young. I still think about him. Do you ever think about your dad? Wonder where he is?'

Rhydian looked up at the darkening sky. 'No,' he lied.

Tom's first impression of the Kafe was that it was colourful. *Very* colourful. The three Ks were buzzing around as more people arrived. Katrina was meeting-and-greeting while Kara and Kay wobbled around on their heels, offering people food. Harry and Shannon had set up in one corner, Shannon's voice filtering over the hubbub as she sang. Tom was just settling down to enjoy the show when Shannon caught his eye and jerked her head towards the door. Tom turned and saw Dr Whitewood coming in. She made a beeline straight for Liam, who was sitting with Jimi and Sam.

Oh no, Tom thought. *This can't be good.*

'What are you doing here?' Liam asked her.

'The day Maddy brought those "wolves" into school,' she said. 'Did anything unusual happen?'

Liam raised his eyebrows. 'Er, yeah. She brought two pet wolves into school.'

'I mean after school,' she said impatiently. 'Because at quarter to five, someone stole that dog chew and the DNA results from my lab. I think it was Tom and Shannon.'

'Nah,' said Liam. 'Can't have been. They were in detention with me, Sam and Jimi.'

'Thanks to you,' Jimi pointed out. 'It was us, Tom, Shan and Rhydian – who legged it after fifteen minutes.'

'Rhydian?' Whitewood repeated.

'Maddy's boyfriend,' Sam reminded her. 'Tall, blond? He ran off when we told him you had the samples.'

Tom shut his eyes. This was not good at all. He had to do something before it was too late . . .

'Hey, guys!' he said, barging up to the table in the hope that he could distract them. 'Shan's really good, isn't she?'

Dr Whitewood ignored him completely. 'Where is Rhydian now?' she asked.

'He's at home tonight,' Tom told her.

'Anyway,' Liam added, 'he couldn't have got to your lab by quarter to five.'

Jimi snorted. 'Not on two legs, anyway!'

Whitewood fixed her attention on Tom. 'Where does he live?' she asked, in a quiet, dangerous voice.

'That's . . . none of your business,' said Tom.

Something in the woman's eyes gleamed. 'Why not?' she asked. 'Does he have something to hide?'

'The Vaughans' place,' said Jimi. 'Over the bridge and turn left. There's a farmhouse about three miles out of town.' He grinned at the doctor and stuck his hand out. 'That's worth a fiver, right?'

Whitewood ignored Jimi and left without another word. Tom pulled out his phone and called Rhydian. 'Whitewood's going to your place,' he hissed, as soon as his friend answered. 'If she gets your DNA . . .'

'I'm on my way . . .' Rhydian said, and hung up.

Shannon was still mid-song, but Tom couldn't wait for her to finish. Thankfully, Shannon could tell something was seriously wrong the minute Tom looked at her. She grimaced, finishing the verse before turning to Harry.

'I'm sorry,' she said to her boyfriend, as she slipped off her stool. 'I'm *so* sorry . . .'

Minutes later they were out of the Kafe and running towards Tom's bike.

Rhydian caught up with Dr Whitewood outside the Vaughans' house. He'd run at full tilt, getting there just in time to see his foster mum tell her that he was staying with a friend. Rhydian cornered the woman as she stepped away from the door.

14

'What are you doing here?' he snarled, right in Whitewood's face. She didn't even flinch.

'I've come to see you,' she said.

Rhydian was about to demand she tell him why when he felt a sharp pain in his arm as Whitewood stabbed him with a syringe. He grabbed at her, but it was too late. Darkness was already swimming up around him, sucking him down until he blacked out.

Rhydian woke up in a cage. He struggled to sit up and realised that he was in the back of a car – Whitewood's Mondeo estate. She was driving. His head ached.

'Wha . . .' he said, still groggy, 'What . . . did you do?'

Whitewood glanced at him in the rear-view mirror, her reflection criss-crossed by the metal grille of the dog guard between them. 'Mild sedative,' she said. 'It'll wear off in a few minutes.'

Through the window, Rhydian saw the moon through the clouds, fat and full and silver. He could feel the Wolfblood pounding in his veins. If he didn't get out soon he was going to change, here in front of her. He tried not to panic, but when they passed the signpost to Stoneybridge he realised that they weren't driving away from the town – they were driving *towards* it.

'What are you doing?' he asked.

'There's a party at the café tonight,' said Whitewood. 'Half the village will be there. I thought we'd say hello. It's the only way to get my life back. They *have* to see you change.'

'No!' With shaking hands, Rhydian fumbled in his pocket for his phone. He just about managed to hit redial. Tom took ages to answer.

'She's locked me in her car,' he managed. 'She's taking me to Stoneybridge . . .'

He felt another surge of the wolf within and dropped the phone. Whitewood threw the car around a corner and then braked so hard that Rhydian went flying.

There was a wolf standing right in the middle of the road, blocking the way.

Dacia.

The wolf stalked slowly towards the car and jumped on to the bonnet, snarling through the windscreen at Whitewood. She jumped down again, shifting back into human form to open the passenger door and slide in beside the stunned driver.

'Get us off the road,' Dacia ordered Whitewood, calmly.

'Why should I?' Whitewood asked.

Dacia snarled, baring her teeth, eyes flashing yellow. Whitewood did as she was told.

'Get me out of here,' Rhydian begged. His blood fizzed, his skin rippled – his atoms rushing, changing, distorting . . .

The wolf within wanted *out*.

Tom and Shannon pelted their way along the road as fast as Tom's bike would carry them. The moon was high in the sky now, so Rhydian must have changed. Where was he? What had Whitewood done with him?

'Shan, look!' Tom shouted. He pointed to two white headlights. They weren't on the road – they were down in a dip in the forest. Tom threw them down the hill, crashing over the uneven ground so quickly Shannon thought her teeth might shake loose from her skull.

It was Whitewood's car all right, but she wasn't in it. She was standing between its headlights, transfixed by the two large wolves sitting in front of her.

'Er . . .' said Tom, as he and Shan got off the bike. 'What happened?'

'Extraordinary,' Whitewood was muttering to herself, as Rhydian and Dacia turned and disappeared into the night. 'Just extraordinary. She made me an offer I couldn't refuse. A . . . job.'

Shannon realised what she meant. 'With . . . Segolia?'

The scientist nodded.

'So . . .' Tom said slowly, into the silence. 'What does that mean?'

Whitewood blinked and then shrugged. 'It means you've nothing to fear from me now. Not if they keep their word.'

'Tom,' said Shannon, her face shining. 'You know what that means, don't you?'

Tom did. They grinned at each other.

'Rhydian!' they both shouted. 'Rhydian! Maddy can come home!'

Somewhere in the distance, a happy wolf howled at the full moon.

Three

Maddy's coming home. She's coming home!

The words rattled around Rhydian's mind as he stood with Shannon and Tom on a quiet forest road not far from the Smiths' house. Maddy and her mum and dad were due to arrive at any minute. They were coming *home*.

But when Dacia's car finally appeared, she was on her own. 'Maddy and her parents have already left,' she told them. 'Canada, by cargo ship. They'll have new identities when they get there.'

Rhydian stared at her. 'Call the ship,' he ordered. 'You can get them back.'

Dacia shook her head. 'It's too late.'

Rhydian felt the anger building in his gut, a slow roll of rage that made him clench his fists so tightly that his nails bit into his palm. He couldn't let Maddy just disappear.

'I'm going after them.' He started walking, trying to think.

'You can't just go to Canada!' Dacia shouted after him.

'Watch me!' he shouted back. He started running. He didn't even stop when he heard Shannon calling his name. He was faster than all of them, except maybe Dacia, and he knew she wouldn't bother coming after him.

He went home first. Mrs Vaughan was in the kitchen, trying to get his two younger foster brothers, Ollie and Joe, ready for school.

'What are you doing back?' she asked him.

'I, er . . .' Rhydian ran up the stairs. 'I . . . forgot my homework!'

He shoved a few clothes in a backpack, grabbed his wallet and, after thinking for a moment, pulled out a drawing he'd done of Maddy and put that in too. If Segolia had given them new identities, she could be called anything by now. This way he had a picture to show people while he searched.

Rhydian went into the kitchen, where Mrs Vaughan was trying to wrestle Ollie into his school tie. Of all the foster mums he'd had, Mrs Vaughan was easily the best. But here he was, about to run off . . . He pulled her into a hug. He wasn't usually one for hugging, but right then he couldn't help it. This was goodbye, even if she didn't know it yet.

'What brought that on?' asked his foster mum, once he'd pulled away.

'Just . . . thanks for looking after me. You'll appreciate her one day, boys,' he said, to the other two. Then he left, quickly, before Mrs Vaughan could use her foster-mum superpowers to work out what was going on.

He hadn't even gone a mile before Tom cycled up behind him with Shannon on the back of his bike.

'Oi!' Tom said, as they climbed off and started walking with him. 'You're being ridiculous.'

'How are you even going to get there?' Shannon asked.

'I'll work something out.'

'Even if you make it to Canada, how are you going to find her?' Tom asked. 'She's in hiding!'

'Wolfbloods can always find their pack,' he told them, still walking.

'Hey,' said Shannon. 'I thought *we* were your pack?'

He stopped, throwing up his hands in exasperation. 'But you're not Wolfbloods!'

Rhydian regretted the words as soon as they were out of his mouth. Tom and Shannon both stopped dead, staring at him. Then, without a word, Tom got on his bike and started cycling back the way he'd come. Shannon followed him.

'Guys!' Rhydian shouted after them, hopelessly. 'I've got to do this!'

'So do it, then!' Tom yelled back.

Rhydian watched his two friends disappear down the road. Part of him wanted to run after them and apologise again. But he didn't.

Shannon and Tom walked into their form room just as Mr Jeffries was reminding them all that they needed to choose their work experience placements.

'Coldwell Lane was flooded again,' Tom explained. 'We had to go round the long way.'

Jeffries sighed. 'And did Rhydian come to school via Coldwell Lane as well?' he asked. 'Because he's late too.'

The question just added to Shannon's annoyance with the day in general. 'How would we know?' she asked.

Mr Jeffries looked a bit surprised. Shannon wasn't usually one to answer back. 'I just thought–'

'We're not his keeper, sir,' she snapped.

There was a chorus of whoops and laughter from the class. Shannon slid into her seat as Tom sat down beside her, both of them glaring at the forms that had been left on their desks.

'Right . . . well, we're thinking about your futures,' Jeffries said, addressing the whole class. 'What are your strengths and weaknesses?'

'Well,' Tom said glumly, under his breath, 'I'm good at losing mates.'

Shannon glanced at him. 'Everything's changing, isn't it?'

He nodded, frowning. 'It's all falling apart.'

Shannon tried to swallow the lump in her throat. There was no way Rhydian would be able to get to Canada – he probably didn't even have enough money to get to the airport, let alone book a flight. She tried to focus on the work experience form. *You're not a proper part of his pack, remember? So what do you care?*

When Jeffries dismissed the class, Shannon and Tom trudged out into the corridor. Shannon had only gone a few steps when she felt a hand on her arm and turned to see Harry.

'Hey, you,' he said, smiling. 'Ready for lunchtime?'

'Ooh,' said Kara, overhearing as the three Ks wafted past. 'What'cha doing at lunchtime, Harry?'

'Something romantic?' Katrina mocked. They all giggled. Shannon really, really wasn't in the mood for this.

'We're just recording some music,' she said. 'It's no big deal.'

Harry frowned. '"No big deal"?' he repeated.

Shannon lost her temper for the second time that morning. 'Yes, Harry! No big deal! There are more important things in life than music!'

The Ks tottered off, laughing, as Jimi Chen looked on with his eyebrows raised. Shannon groaned inwardly.

'I'm sorry,' she said to Harry, who was looking more than a little confused.

'If you don't want to do this . . .' he said.

'No,' she told him. 'I'll see you in the music room at lunchtime.'

Harry hesitated, as if trying to find something else to say. In the end he gave up and kissed her on the cheek before disappearing off down the corridor.

Tom raised his eyebrows. 'What was all that about, Shan?'

'Look,' she said, feeling as if she needed to explain herself even though she really didn't want to. 'I like singing, and I like Harry, but we want different things, and he can't see that because all he cares about is my voice.'

'Maybe you should tell him this, instead of me?' Tom suggested.

Shannon gave him a look. 'Or maybe I've lost enough friends for one day?'

She knew she'd have to, though. She and Harry just weren't meant to be.

Rhydian had picked a direction and was running in it. He'd wolf out when he was far enough away from

Stoneybridge – four legs could travel faster than two. Liverpool was a long way off, but Rhydian knew he could make it. Maddy had taken a cargo ship – that was what Dacia had said. Well, if they had, then so could he. Maybe he could get a job on one that was also headed for Canada. If not, he could always stow away.

He was caught off balance by a scent he recognised. Wolfbloods! Skidding to a halt, Rhydian scanned the woods. Shapes moved amid the shadows cast by the morning sun filtering through the leaves overhead. Then he spotted them – both in human form.

Aran and Meinir.

They turned and ran. He gave chase as they went deeper into the forest. Rhydian wondered if he were being led into an ambush, but he kept going, needing answers more than he needed to be safe. Meinir dropped out of sight as Aran suddenly stopped and turned back. The wild Wolfblood was standing beside a pile of branches that looked as if they had been deliberately arranged to hide something. Rhydian ran around it and saw a figure crouching in the leaves.

'Mum!'

Ceri straightened up, a worried look on her face. Beyond her, Rhydian could see a bundle of clothes, hidden beneath the branches. Then he saw the flash of red hair.

25

Jana!

'What happened?' he asked.

'She's been shot,' Ceri told him. 'A traveller was on our territory – he was hunting Wolfbloods, with a gun. Jana tried to draw him away, but she wasn't quick enough.'

Jana's eyes were open, but she was deathly pale. He knelt beside his friend and gently pulled her into his arms.

'All right,' he said, lifting her up. 'Follow me.'

Four

Rhydian took them to the safest place he could think of – Maddy's house. He carried Jana as gently as he could.

'I thought it would heal,' Ceri told him, as they laid Jana on the sofa inside. 'I have the remedies to prevent infection . . .'

Aran stuck his face close to Rhydian's. 'The tame wolves – will they help?'

Rhydian shook his head. 'They're not here any more. Doctor Whitewood found out about them – they're on their way to Canada.'

Jana shifted painfully. 'How long has Maddy been gone?' she whispered.

'They left a week after you did.'

'Oh, Rhydian,' Jana said, her voice sad. 'I'm sorry.'

'We brought our alpha here for nothing,' Meinir snarled, pacing back and forth, agitated.

'No,' said Ceri. 'No – Rhydian can help. Can't you?'

'Course he can,' Jana whispered, with a smile.

'All right,' he said, sounding far more sure of himself than he felt. 'Let's get her upstairs.' No one moved, and it took him a moment to realise that the wild Wolfbloods had no idea what stairs were. He pointed. 'Up there!'

As they did as he'd told them, Rhydian dug his phone out of his pocket and sent a quick text to Shannon and Tom: NEED HELP. MADDY'S HOUSE. URGENT!

He'd just have to hope they'd come. He ran upstairs to find that Aran and Meinir had chosen Maddy's room. Rhydian had to pause for a second before he could make himself go in. Everything in that room still smelled of *her* . . .

Don't be an idiot. Get on with it, he told himself. *Jana needs you!*

'So how can you help?' Aran demanded.

'Hospitals,' Jana whispered weakly, her head against Maddy's pillow. 'With you doing the talking, we could go there.'

'No, we can't,' Rhydian told her. 'The hospital will call the police. Do blood tests, find out what you are . . .'

'Then what *are* you going to do?' asked Meinir. 'We must return her to the pack!'

'Aran, Meinir – go and wait outside,' said Jana. 'Ceri will stay with me.'

28

Once she was sure they've gone, Jana fixed Ceri with a serious look. 'Tell him the truth.'

Rhydian's mum took a deep breath. 'The bullet is too deep for me to remove. It's poisoning her. If it we don't get it out . . .' she trailed off.

'I'll die,' said Jana. 'Aran and Meinir don't know. They'll replace me as pack leader if they think I won't live. It's their nature to need a strong alpha.'

Rhydian was too shocked to say anything. He sank down on to the bed, taking her hand. Jana squeezed it gently. He tried to smile but he couldn't. Rhydian couldn't bear to lose Maddy *and* Jana.

Tom and Shannon arrived as fast as they could, running the gauntlet of a school break-out. Shannon ran straight upstairs to see Jana, but Rhydian stopped Tom.

'Tom, you need to get your mum here. It's Jana's only chance.'

'Are you insane?' Tom said. 'My mum won't do that. You know her, she's all about rules. She'll call the police and then an ambulance. Which you need to do, right now.'

But Rhydian couldn't do that. Even with Jana's life in the balance, giving up the Wolfblood secret was too huge to risk. So he called Dacia.

'I need a Wolfblood doctor,' he told her. 'Please, it's an emergency. You have to send someone right now.'

'All right,' Dacia told him. 'I'll see what I can do.'

But in the end, even the might of Segolia failed him. Dacia arrived, but the doctor was with another patient, apparently. Rhydian was desperate and tensions in the house were running high. The wild Wolfbloods could tell that Jana was getting weaker. They hated having the humans around, not to mention being indoors. When Aran heard Tom and Shannon chatting with Jana and telling her she should stay for a while even once she was better, he nearly lost it completely.

'Get away from my alpha,' he snarled at them, barging into Maddy's bedroom. 'Stop tempting her to stay in your world!'

Rhydian stepped in, trying to placate the situation. 'No one's tempting anyone anywhere . . .'

'You're lying!' Aran turned on him, pointing at Tom and Shannon. 'That is why you brought *them* here!'

'You came for our help,' Rhydian reminded him. 'That's what you're getting.'

'Rhydian!'

Shannon's scared voice cut through the argument.

Everyone looked at Jana to see that she'd slumped against Shannon, eyes closed and skin deathly pale. Ceri rushed to Jana's side.

'She's alive,' said Rhydian's mother, 'but only just.'

'This is not right,' growled Meinir. 'She should breathe her last in the wild, like the wolf she is.'

Rhydian blinked. 'A wolf?' he repeated, as a thought popped into his head.

'Don't write me off yet, Meinir,' Jana whispered, struggling to open her eyes. 'You . . . are *my* . . . pack . . .'

'Like a *wolf*!' Rhydian said. He pulled out his phone and dialled a number. 'I've got an emergency,' he said to the voice on the other end of the line. This idea had to work, because it was Jana's last hope.

Once he knew help was coming, he explained to Jana and Ceri what they would have to do. It was dangerous, but they didn't have any choice. Jana was dying, and this was their last chance to save her. They carried her downstairs, wrapped in one of Maddy's blankets, and laid her on the kitchen table.

'Are you sure you can do this?' Rhydian whispered in her ear.

Jana's eyes fluttered open. 'If Ceri can, I can,' she said.

There was a noise outside – a car pulling into the

driveway. 'It's time,' Rhydian told Jana. She nodded weakly.

Outside, Rhydian found Dr Loseley climbing out of her car, carrying a big black medical bag.

'Thanks for coming,' he told her, trying to delay her for a few minutes.

'Where's the patient? It sounded urgent . . .'

Rhydian nodded and led her back inside. 'On the table,' he said, pointing to where Jana lay: wolf-Jana, not human-Jana.

The vet stopped dead. 'That's . . . not a dog.'

Rhydian swallowed. 'I may not have told you the whole truth . . . We found her in the woods and called Doctor Jones . . .'

Ceri stepped forward, holding out her hand. 'I am Ceri Jones,' she explained. 'I'm a zoologist – I study wolves. When I saw what had happened, I said they must call a vet.'

'She's been shot,' Rhydian said.

Dr Loseley stared nervously at the wolf. 'What a shame,' she said. 'Such a beautiful animal too . . .' She put down her bag and opened it, pulling out a vial of clear liquid and quickly filling a syringe. 'It might be better if you all wait outside. I'm sorry, but this is better than allowing her to suffer any more.'

'Hold on,' said Tom. 'Is that what I think it is?'

'That's a wild animal,' said the vet firmly. 'It knows it's dying – otherwise you would have been attacked.'

'You can't just put her down,' said Shannon, her voice shaking.

'I have no choice,' said Loseley. She went to Jana, but Ceri grabbed her hands.

'Look at me,' Ceri said. 'She won't hurt you. She just wants to meet you – to get your scent. Come.' She took the syringe from Dr Loseley. 'Put out your fists. Gently – don't be scared. Let her sniff you . . .'

The vet trembled as she held her hands out to Jana's wolf-self. Jana sniffed the woman's hands, whining gently.

'You're a healer,' Ceri told Loseley softly. 'It's a gift – it's what you were born to do. Take the bullet out and clean the wound.'

Loseley nodded. 'O-OK. I have to do this quickly . . . You stay and help. The rest of you – please give us some space.'

They all went down into the den in the cellar and waited. Aran and Meinir curled up on the straw. Rhydian looked at Tom and Shannon, sitting together on the stairs. They weren't Wolfblood, but they were still family. What had he been thinking, trying to run off without them?

'I'm sorry. I shouldn't have said what I said this morning,' Rhydian said. 'It wasn't fair. Of course we're a pack.'

Shannon smiled. 'Apology accepted.'

Rhydian looked at Tom, wondering if he was going to hold a grudge. 'I'm just a big softy,' Tom sighed eventually. 'You know that.'

Rhydian grinned.

Wolf-Jana slept peacefully as Dr Loseley operated. Ceri didn't leave Jana's side for a moment – it was too dangerous. With Jana under anaesthetic, her body could slip back into human form at any moment. Ceri whispered to Jana, words of their ancient language calculated to soothe and calm.

Later, once the vet had gone, Ceri and Aran carried Jana up to Maddy's bedroom, where she changed back into human form. She was still pale, but her eyes were already brighter. She was on the mend.

'The poison's gone,' she said. 'I can feel it.'

Tom tapped Shannon on the arm. 'We should get home before the school rings to check up on us.'

'Thank you,' said Aran, surprising everyone. 'Both of you. She would not have survived without you.'

No one said anything for a moment. It was a big thing for Aran to admit, and they all knew it.

Shannon smiled at him. 'Thank *you*,' she said. 'You brought her all the way here.'

The Wolfbloods and the humans smiled at each other.

They had saved Jana together, and wasn't that what she had always wanted? To have humans and Wolfbloods working together, side by side?

Five

It was dark. Tom wouldn't usually be heading up to the Smiths' place so late, but Jana's bullet wound was taking a long time to heal and she was bored. Tom was bringing her his old laptop and a handful of DVDs that he thought might help.

Hopping over a gate, he was taking a shortcut across a field when he heard something. He swung around, his torch slicing through the night, but there was nothing there. He carried on walking, but then he heard it again. There was definitely something in this field with him . . . He started to hurry.

The night was suddenly cracked open by lights so bright he was blinded. Tom threw up his arm to shield his eyes. It was two four-wheel drives. Then something rammed into him, knocking him to the ground.

'Get off!' he yelled, struggling with whatever it was.

The lights came closer as the cars revved their engines and rolled right at him. In the harsh white shine, Tom realised who had attacked him.

'Rhydian!'

'Come on!' His friend dragged him up. 'Run!'

The cars were coming at them. Tom ran, dodging behind Rhydian and Aran, who had appeared out of nowhere. They headed for the fence at the end of the field, scrambling over it and into the forest. They stumbled down a slope and then Rhydian dragged Tom behind the wide trunk of an old oak. They crouched there, breathing hard, hoping no one would come after them. No one did.

'Do you know what would have happened if you'd got caught?' Tom said angrily, once they'd made it back to the house.

Aran growled at him. 'Wolfbloods know how to hunt unseen!'

'That wasn't hunting, that was stealing,' Tom told him, pointing at the sack. He looked up as Ceri and Jana made their way down the stairs. 'They were poaching,' he told Jana, expecting her to be as outraged as he was – but she wasn't. She knew, he realised. So did Ceri. They all knew.

'Jana needs red meat,' Ceri explained. 'She won't heal on scraps and human food.'

'So you just stole it?'

'You've no right to judge us,' Aran growled.

'Why,' Tom spat back, 'because I'm not "Wolfblood"?'

'Because we weren't the ones who got seen,' said Rhydian, obviously angry too.

'You were seen?' Ceri asked, worried.

37

'And he'd have been caught if I hadn't gone back for him,' Rhydian added, as if everything that had happened so far that evening was Tom's fault.

'The only reason that farmer was even out there was because he was trying to catch you,' Tom snapped back, angry too.

'OK, OK,' Jana said, trying to calm everyone down. 'This isn't Tom's fault. He's right. We're guests here. We don't steal. We get by on what we can find in the woods,' she said firmly.

Tom shot a triumphant look at Rhydian, who scowled back.

'Honestly, Shan, Rhydian was acting as if it was all my fault,' Tom griped next morning as he told Shannon what had happened. He rummaged through his locker. 'I can't find my planner,' he muttered.

'I think you're taking it a bit personally,' Shannon soothed, as Rhydian turned up.

'All right, mate?' Tom asked.

Rhydian just blanked him.

From there the day got rapidly worse. Tom had only just sat down when Liam threw a wad of paper at him, hitting him on the head.

'Oi,' Tom said, turning around. 'What's your problem?'

Liam held up Tom's missing planner.

'My planner! Where did you find it?'

'My dad's field,' Liam said. 'Where you left it.'

For a minute Tom didn't know what to say. Out of the corner of his eye he saw Rhydian turn around. 'I haven't been in your dad's field.'

Liam stood up. 'Then how'd it get there?'

'I dunno. Someone probably nicked it.'

'You think I'm that stupid?' Liam said, clenching his fists.

'Whoa,' said Mr Jeffries, walking in just as Liam was about to swing his first punch. 'What's going on?'

'My dad caught Tom poaching, sir,' said Liam. 'He saw him.'

'How?' asked Tom. 'He's never even met me!'

Liam showed Jeffries the planner. 'He left that behind, sir.'

Mr Jeffries glanced at the planner and then at Tom. 'Where were you last night, Tom?'

Tom had no idea what to say. 'I was – I was at . . .'

Shannon stood up. 'He was with me,' she blurted. 'We – we're going out. I told Tom I didn't want people to know, because I've only just split up with Harry. He was with me.'

The whole class burst out laughing and whistling.

'All right, all right,' shouted Jeffries, over the noise. 'That's enough melodrama for one day. Settle down.'

Liam skulked back to his seat, throwing Tom a death glare.

'Liam's not buying it,' Rhydian warned Tom and Shannon, as they made their way to the canteen for lunch. To be honest, Rhydian wasn't surprised. His two friends didn't seem to be putting much effort into their 'couple' act. In drama, Rhydian had been paired with Katrina, who was more interested in finding out the gossip about Shannon and Tom than she was doing any work. The rumour was that Shannon had started going out with Tom before she'd split up with Harry, and now it was all anyone wanted to talk about.

'You think we want to be doing this?' Shannon hissed.

'This is pointless if you can't make him believe you were together last night,' Rhydian said. 'If you can't, he'll carry on thinking Tom was the poacher, won't he?'

Tom raised his hands, exasperated. 'Well, what do you want us to do about it?'

'Be more couple-y,' Rhydian suggested, leaving them to go and get his lunch.

He watched as Shannon and Tom sat facing each other with their trays. Tom half-heartedly offered Shannon a bit of his lunch on the end of his fork. This was never going to work. They looked too awkward with each other. Still, everyone – including Liam – was watching.

Then Tom leaned in across the table for a kiss. For a second it looked as if Shannon wasn't going to go with it, but she leaned in too. Their lips were about to touch when Harry Averwood appeared beside their table, looking about as angry as Rhydian had ever seen him. The entire canteen abruptly went silent.

'Can I talk to you?' Harry said to Shannon.

She nodded, her face miserable as she followed him out of the room. Then Rhydian saw Liam slip out after them. Rhydian shot Tom a look and then followed himself.

Six

They had all disappeared by the time he got outside, but Rhydian's wolf senses told him that they were in the girls' changing rooms. Sneaking in, he could hear Shannon and Harry talking quietly. Rhydian could smell that Liam was there too – he'd hidden inside the girls' showers so he could hear what was going on.

'Were you two-timing me with Tom?' Harry was asking.

'I didn't cheat on you, if that's what you mean,' Shannon said, her voice hurt.

'Quick turnaround though, wasn't it?' Harry asked. 'Just be straight with me, Shannon. Please.'

There was a pause as Shannon struggled with what to say. Rhydian saw Liam peeking out of the showers, filming Harry and Shannon with his phone.

'I want to tell you something,' Shannon was telling Harry. 'But you have to swear – you can't tell anyone.'

Rhydian panicked as Liam leaned forward eagerly. *She's going to tell him the truth,* he thought, *and Liam will hear!* Pulling out his own phone, Rhydian sent Shannon a text.

42

'Last night, Tom was somewhere he shouldn't have been and I . . . I gave him an alibi,' she was saying. 'I told everyone we were together, and it sort of . . .'

Rhydian heard the beep as his text reached her phone.

'Sorry,' Shannon muttered, pulling it out and reading what it said:

LIAM IS LISTENING

'Um,' Rhydian heard her say, obviously now completely thrown.

'Shannon?' Harry asked.

There was a pause, and then Shannon said., 'Look. The truth is, Tom and I *are* going out.'

'So what?' Harry said. 'That other bit just now was a lie?'

'Yeah,' said Shannon. 'I'm sorry, Harry. I . . . I didn't want you to think that I'd do something like that.'

'But you did,' said Harry, in disgust.

Suddenly two younger girls appeared.

'Oi,' said one of them to Harry. 'You can't be in here!'

'I'm gone,' Harry said, walking away.

'Harry – I'm sorry,' Shannon said, following. 'Please . . .'

Harry ignored her. Rhydian was about to leave too, when a shriek came from the shower stalls. The girls had found Liam.

'You creep!' yelled one of the girls, snatching his phone. 'Were you going to film us?'

'No!' said Liam, trying to grab the phone.

'Right,' said the girl, holding it up. 'If you want this back, you have to say the magic words. Repeat after me . . . "I, Liam Hunter, promise never to spy in the girls' changing rooms again like a massive, creepy weirdo".'

Rhydian grinned. Pulling out his own phone again, he flicked on the video and held it up. This was too good an opportunity to miss!

'I wasn't spying!' Liam protested.

'And those weren't the magic words,' the girl pointed out. 'Do you want this back, or not?'

'All right, all right,' Liam sulked. 'I, Liam Hunter, promise never to spy in the girls' changing rooms again . . . like a . . . a massive . . . creepy . . . weirdo."

'Better,' said the girl.

Jana knew that Aran wasn't happy. He missed Meinir – she had returned to the pack to give them news of Jana's recovery and although they expected her to return once this task had been completed, her brother seemed lost without her. He hated living indoors too. Like all wild Wolfbloods, he was afraid that being comfortable would tame him.

'This place is a cage,' he'd told her, just the day before, when he'd found Jana watching one of the films Tom had brought her. Then he'd accused Jana of preferring soft, human ways to the ways of the pack.

It wasn't true, Jana told herself. Just because she liked films and beds and flushing toilets, that didn't mean she didn't love the way the pack lived too. But to Aran, accepting any of those things was a sign that she was weak, which was dangerous whether it was true or not. An alpha who was thought to be weak would be challenged and replaced by someone stronger. Look what had happened to Jana's father, Alric.

Which was why Jana was currently in the Smiths' garden, ignoring the pain in her side and trying to walk without her crutch. Aran and Ceri were watching. Aran was smiling, but Ceri looked anxious.

'You don't have to do this,' Ceri told her.

Jana tried to keep her face brave. She reached the old apple tree, turned around and started back again.

'It's getting better,' Ceri said, surprised.

'Then we move on,' said Aran firmly. 'Tomorrow.'

Ceri looked at him as if he were mad. 'She can't travel yet!'

'She will get better in the wild,' said Aran. 'The pack can hunt for her.'

They were talking about her as if she were a cub that needed looking after, not an alpha who led an entire pack. 'You forget yourself,' Jana told Aran.

'No, you forget,' snapped Aran. 'You know what happens to Wolfbloods who stay too long.'

'Then go,' Jana barked. 'If you're so afraid of this place, then go!'

'Jana,' Ceri warned, 'don't be foolish.'

'He thinks I want to keep us here!' Jana shouted. 'He's been fighting to leave ever since we arrived!'

'If I don't, you'll never go back!' said Aran. 'A wild pack needs a wild leader.'

Jana shook her head. 'I stay until I am healed. You can do what you want.'

'I didn't risk my life to bring you here, to watch you grow tame!'

Jana snarled, feeling the wolf rising as her eyes flashed yellow. How dare he challenge her so openly? She stepped towards him, baring her teeth, and Aran backed down, showing the submission she was due. Then he turned and ran, heading for the forest.

Jana stalked back into the house, Ceri on her tail.

'If you send him back without us, he and Meinir will try to take the pack,' Ceri warned.

Jana didn't believe her. 'Aran is afraid, not disloyal.'

'I don't trust him.'

'He doesn't trust me!'

'And?' Ceri asked. 'Are his fears founded?'

Jana sank down on to the sofa. 'I will not betray the pack.'

'I know that. You adapt, you accept, and you embrace two worlds, but where I see open-mindedness Aran only sees vulnerability and danger. Prove to him you know your mind, and he will trust it.'

Jana nodded. Ceri was right. She needed to reassure Aran. 'Will you go after him?'

Ceri reached out to squeeze Jana's hand. Then she was gone.

Rhydian was leaving school after the final bell when he realised that something was badly wrong. It wasn't so much a scent as a sense – something in the air, calling to him.

'Rhydian?' Shannon asked. 'What is it?'

He didn't answer, striking out towards the school field instead. Eolas would tell him. He dropped to his knees in a daze and pressed his hands into the ground.

'Oops,' said Shannon, pulling Tom to her so they could shield what Rhydian was doing from the rest of the school.

Rhydian sank into Eolas, feeling all his senses sharpen. He could see everything, smell everything . . . He searched for the thread that had reached out to him, realising that it was Ceri. He saw her running – chasing something – then saw her stop. She heard something snap and stepped backwards, but it was too late. Ropes closed around her, dragging her into the air as she flailed.

It was no good – she hung there, trapped, howling for help.

Rhydian stood up with a gasp, the last vestiges of Eolas flooding away from him like a tide.

'What's happened?' Tom asked.

'Mum,' said Rhydian shortly. He started to run, not even stopping to explain, or pausing to notice that Liam was watching him. Rhydian raced across the school grounds and out into the forest, following his mother's scent.

He found her, just as Eolas had shown him, caught in a trap that had pulled her several feet off the ground.

'What happened?' he asked.

'I don't know,' Ceri told him.

Rhydian saw movement in the branches above and realised that Aran was climbing up to the knot. 'Look out,' the wild Wolfblood called, and before Rhydian could stop him, he'd severed the rope, sending Ceri crashing to the ground.

'Oh, well done,' Rhydian shouted.

'I'm all right,' Ceri said, as she got to her feet.

'What are you doing out here, anyway?' Rhydian asked. 'Come on, let's get back.'

They met Jana halfway back to the farmhouse – she'd heard Ceri's howl for help too, and had done her best to assist her despite her injuries.

'Are you all right?' Jana asked Ceri.

'Yes,' said Ceri. 'Aran came to my aid.'

'Do you doubt my loyalty?' Aran asked, at the look of surprise on Jana's face.

'Do you doubt mine?' Jana countered, as the two faced each other. When he didn't answer, she sighed. 'I know what scares you, Aran. It scared me too once. But tame . . . tame isn't something that happens to you, it's something you choose. I choose our pack, and I choose you to get us home. But if we don't trust each other, we won't make it.'

Aran thought for a long moment, and then made as if to get down on one knee to show Jana that he was submissive to her leadership. But she stopped him.

'I want trust,' she told him, 'not allegiance.'

After a pause, Aran held out his hand for a human-style handshake. Jana was astonished. 'Apparently,' Aran told her, 'it is both greeting and agreement.'

At his words, Jana grinned, and they shook hands.

Rhydian breathed a sigh of relief.

They all thought the danger had passed. Tom and Shannon rode up to the house and everyone sat in the kitchen while Ceri told them her story. Then Rhydian told Jana that Tom and Shannon were a couple.

'You're going out?' she repeated, incredulous.

'We were just pretending,' said Tom awkwardly. 'To cover for the other night.'

Jana laughed. 'Well . . . thanks, I guess,' she said, still smiling.

A second later her smile had gone and Jana was on her feet, sniffing the air. Aran and Ceri were alert, Aran growling at the window. Rhydian straightened up, recognising the scent.

'Liam,' he warned. 'Everyone – hide.'

'Tom, Shannon,' came Liam's voice, as they all ducked away from the windows. 'I know you're in there!'

'Just stay down,' Rhydian whispered. 'He's not going to break in.'

Jana didn't listen. She went to the door and opened it. Liam looked shocked to see her.

'Jana?' he said.

'Come inside,' she said.

Liam hesitated, then did as he was told. He looked around at everyone gathered there before looking back at Ceri.

'It was you,' he said, pulling a video camera out of his pocket. 'In the trap. I filmed it. I've got proof now. It's you lot who have been taking our lambs, isn't it?'

There was a moment of silence and Rhydian stepped forward. 'It was me, Liam. It's nothing to do with them. They didn't ask me to do it,' Rhydian said, looking squarely at Liam. 'No one else is going to take the fall but me.'

Liam pulled out his phone. 'I'm calling the police.'

'Sure,' Rhydian said casually, getting his own phone out of his pocket and thumbing open the video app. 'You can do that . . . but . . .'

He played the video of Liam getting caught in the girls' changing room so that the whole room could hear it.

'I, Liam Hunter, promise never to spy in the girls' changing rooms again like a . . . a massive creepy weirdo . . .'

Liam's cheeks burned red. 'You were spying on me.'

Rhydian shrugged. 'Apparently you were spying on them. Destroy your evidence and this stays between us.'

'That's blackmail,' Liam protested.

'Yeah,' admitted Rhydian. 'Give me the SD card, don't tell anyone they're here – and this won't go online.'

Liam stared at him for a moment, furious. Then he handed over the SD card and stormed out. The others breathed in relief. As guilty as Rhydian felt over the blackmail, at least they were safe. For now.

Seven

Rhydian and Tom were standing in Stoneybridge's square on Saturday morning. Tom was trying to persuade Rhydian that they were going to have fun at the Manchester United match that Tom was dragging him to. Rhydian wasn't convinced.

'I'm not even a Man U fan,' he protested, much to Tom's chagrin.

'If you say that when we're in the stands,' Tom warned him, 'I do not know you.'

Rhydian was no longer listening. He sniffed. There was that unmistakeable scent – the one that told him there was another Wolfblood nearby. He spotted a guy leaning over one of the bins. He was scruffy and unshaven, in a crumpled old hat – and he was most definitely a Wolfblood. The man looked up, as if sensing that someone was watching him. Then he scarpered.

'Hey!' Rhydian shouted. 'Wait – I just want to talk to you!'

Rhydian gave chase as the Wolfblood headed straight for the woods.

'Rhydian!' Tom shouted after him, in mild despair.

The man crashed through the woods, weaving this way and that in an attempt to shake Rhydian off. Eventually he realised it was hopeless and stopped dead, turning around with his hands raised.

'All right, all right,' he said, out of breath. 'You got me.'

Rhydian came closer and as he did, they both seemed to sense something at the same time. Something familiar, something . . . shared.

Tom chose that moment to catch up with them. 'Rhydian!' he wheezed, out of breath.

The stranger blinked. 'Rhydian?'

Rhydian could hardly believe it. 'Dad?'

Tom looked from one to the other. He had the feeling he'd be taking Shannon to the match, instead. So what if they'd only just staged a massive 'break-up' in front of the whole school? They could still hang out . . . right?

Tom sighed. Being friends with Wolfbloods made life so difficult sometimes.

Dacia watched as Ceri applied one of her potions to Jana's wound. 'It's phenomenal,' she said, 'what your herbal remedies can do when combined with antibiotics.' She passed Jana a packet of pills. 'This is your last course. Make sure you take them all.'

Jana smiled. 'Thank you – I'm in your debt.'

'Well, actually,' Dacia told her, 'there is something you could do for me . . . The potions. Segolia would love to research them.'

Ceri's glare was enough to send a shiver down Dacia's spine. 'They are a pack secret,' she snapped.

'Which,' Jana said, her voice holding a warning, 'I will discuss sharing with others on our return. If the pack agrees, I'll let you know.'

Ceri growled.

'I said we'd discuss it,' Jana insisted, but Ceri ran out of the room. Jana glanced at Aran and they both followed.

Dacia heard them all going out of the front door. She looked at Ceri's bag, abandoned on the bed and full of all her Wolfblood remedies. Now would be the perfect time to take a few samples – they'd never know, so how could it possibly hurt? Then she heard what was going on outside. Going to the window, Dacia was shocked to see someone she hadn't expected to see. Pulling out her phone, she stepped away from the window and called a number.

Rhydian watched his mother growl angrily at his dad. He'd assumed that Ceri would be as pleased to see Gerwyn as he'd been, but here she was baring her teeth and yellowing her eyes as if her wolf was going to appear at any minute.

'Mum,' he tried, 'calm down! He's just come to talk to you.'

'He'd never turn up just to see me!' Ceri spat.

'That's not true!' Gerwyn said earnestly. 'I'd like you back in my life. Both of you. I want you to grant me Enouwian.'

Rhydian had no idea what he was talking about. 'What's Enouwian?'

'If a traitor wants to rejoin the pack, he must be forgiven by those he's wronged,' Aran explained.

'It's a ritual,' Jana added.

'One I'll never grant,' Ceri growled. 'You're not welcome here. Go!'

'Mum, please,' Rhydian begged her. 'Just listen to him!'

Jana stepped forward. 'Ceri. Go back inside.' At first it seemed as if his mum might disobey the order, but after a bit more angry glaring she disappeared back into the house. Jana looked at Gerwyn. 'I'll talk to her. Stay here.'

'Thank you,' said Gerwyn.

'I'm not doing it for you,' Jana told him, before she vanished too.

'Um,' said Rhydian. 'Aran? How about some nice rabbit for dinner?'

'Actually,' Gerwyn piped up, 'I'm not too keen on

rabbit these days, to be honest with you. See if you could bag a pheasant? Or a wood pigeon would be fine . . .' He took a step back as Aran nearly went for him. Then, as the wild Wolfblood took the hunting sack and headed for the forest, he added, 'Never did have a sense of humour did he, that one? Not many of them do.'

Rhydian couldn't help but smile. 'So why have you come back now?' he asked.

Gerwyn shrugged. 'It's quite simple really. I gave you up for what I thought I wanted. Cushy job. House. Car. Nice holidays . . . Oh yes, Segolia looked after me really well. And then . . . One day . . .'

'What?'

'I realised they weren't what I thought they were. You give your life to a pack, the pack looks after you. That's how it works, yeah? Well, what if you did do that – gave your life to a pack, and suddenly the pack turn against you?'

'So they just sacked you?'

'It makes you realise what you lost, you know. Where your real family are.'

'You know I have a little brother, don't you?' Rhydian asked. 'His name's Bryn.'

Gerwyn was obviously shocked. 'No,' he said, quietly. 'No, I didn't know. Is . . . Is the father still around, like?'

Rhydian looked up at him. Surely he'd known that he had another son? 'No,' he said pointedly. 'No, he left. At about the same time you did, funnily enough.'

His dad stared at him for a moment, realising what Rhydian was saying . 'Oh,' he said. 'I didn't . . . I didn't know.' He stared into the forest for a few minutes, and then he said, 'I've got to go.'

Rhydian was shocked. He'd only just met his dad again – and Gerwyn had just discovered he had another son he'd never even known about. Would he walk out, just like that? 'Wait,' he said. 'If you can't stay around for her, stay around for me? At least for a while?'

Dacia used her wolf hearing when Jana and Ceri came back into the kitchen. Their urgent tones rose up to her like echoes amplified in a cave.

'He walked out on his unborn child!' Ceri said, her voice full of emotion. 'I can't just forgive and forget.'

'If you can't forgive him, then maybe Rhydian can,' said Jana. 'He has a right to know his own father, doesn't he?'

'It's Rhydian I'm thinking of!' Ceri hissed. 'He'll get hurt!'

'Rhydian's not a cub any more – you can't decide for him,' the pack leader pointed out calmly. 'Ceri, if Gerwyn means nothing to you, then what's the big deal about hearing him out?'

57

Ceri huffed a little at that, but seemed to see the point Jana was making. She went back outside. 'One night,' Dacia heard Ceri telling Rhydian. 'Just for one night – then he'll have to make other arrangements.'

Dacia got up. Good – Gerwyn was going to be here for a bit longer. At least that meant she wouldn't be bringing Segolia security here on a wild goose chase. She saw Ceri's bag again, and bit her lip for a minute before making a decision.

It's not stealing, she told herself, as she quickly took one of the vials and opened it, using the dropper to transfer some into a sample carrier she'd brought with her. *It's only a few drops – and think of the good Segolia can do with it. Think of the advances in research . . . Wolfbloods and humans could both benefit . . .*

'Glad to see you're embracing civilisation, Ceri,' she heard Gerwyn say, as he came into the kitchen. Dacia's heart jumped – she needed to be quick. She opened another of Ceri's vials, adding another few drops to her sample box.

'I'm not,' said Ceri. 'We're going back to the wild in a few days.'

'Look,' said Gerwyn, trying again. 'Rhydian told me about Bryn. I am sorry. I didn't know. I know that what I did was wrong. But . . . we were a family once.'

'The pack is my family now,' Dacia heard Ceri say coldly. 'If Rhydian wants you in his life, fine, he can grant Enouwian. I won't.'

There came the sound of footsteps, and Dacia realised with a jolt that Ceri and Jana were coming up the stairs and stuffed everything away. Ceri arrived in the doorway, eyes flashing angrily after her encounter with Rhydian's dad. She took one look at Dacia and another at her bag and then sniffed, growling. Dacia backed away. Ceri knew exactly what she'd done.

'I – I just took a few samples,' she confessed, as Jana appeared at Ceri's side. 'It was only a few drops. I didn't mean any harm,' Dacia said, genuinely scared as the two Wolfbloods advanced slowly across the room, teeth bared and snarling. 'I'll put them all back! Rhydian,' she shouted. 'Rhydian – help!'

Suddenly Rhydian was in the room, eyes burning yellow. 'Enough!' he ordered Ceri and Jana. 'My territory – my rules. *Enough!*'

They backed down. Dacia sighed with relief, but when she saw the disgusted look on Rhydian's face, her heart sank.

'I saved you from Whitewood,' Dacia reminded him desperately. 'And did the company thank me? No. They said I put them in an impossible situation – because they'd had to give her a job.'

'That doesn't give you the right to take what isn't yours,' said Rhydian.

'Mr Kincaid runs our research and development,' Dacia tried again. 'He said your remedies could benefit mankind as well as Wolfbloods . . .'

'So he asked you to steal them?'

'No. But I don't call it stealing, I call it sharing. Returning the favours I've done for you.'

Rhydian looked at her, his eyes grave. 'I think you should leave.'

They all followed Dacia down into the kitchen, where Rhydian's dad was rooting nosily through the cupboards.

'Hello, Gerwyn,' said Dacia.

'Wait – you know my dad?' Rhydian asked, shocked.

'Yeah, I do,' she said, staring hard at Gerwyn. 'Do you want to tell them why you're really here?'

Gerwyn said nothing.

'No?' she said, stepping forward as Gerwyn backed away. 'All right, I will. Gerwyn's on the run for embezzling millions from Segolia. That's why he's shown up here now. He's looking for a place to hide. It's why they sent me to your school in the first place,' Dacia told Rhydian. 'To see if you'd been in contact with him.'

Rhydian was silent for a minute, looking between his

dad and Dacia. 'So . . . you've *both* been using me.' He stalked out of the kitchen, heading for the den.

'Rhydian! Let me explain!' called Gerwyn urgently. He turned to Ceri and pointed at Dacia. 'Don't let her leave!'

Dacia suddenly felt very cold indeed.

Eight

Rhydian paced the den, anger bubbling up under his shoulder blades. Why couldn't people just be what they said they were, instead of lying all the time?

'It's true they're after me,' his dad admitted. 'But I was set up, I swear.'

'Then why didn't you just tell me that?'

Gerwyn sighed. 'Everything I said today is true . . . I just didn't tell you the *whole* truth.'

'Then tell me now. *Everything*. What did you do?'

'I didn't *do* anything! I just worked in accounts!' His dad took a deep breath. 'A while back, I stumbled across a discrepancy in the company books. Money unaccounted for, linked to something called Cerberus. It wasn't listed anywhere. I ran it by my supervisor, who said he'd check it out. The next thing I know its three o'clock in the morning and a security team's banging on my door.'

'What did they say?'

'I wasn't going to stick around to find out! Victoria Sweeney doesn't call in the middle of the night for a friendly chat.'

'Who's Victoria Sweeney?'

Gerwyn made a sound in his throat. 'Head of security at Segolia. Someone you don't want to cross. So I climbed out of my bedroom window, shinned down a drainpipe and ran. They've been looking for me ever since.'

Aran pounced on another rabbit, twisting its neck so quickly that the creature didn't have time to scream. He shoved it in his sack. That made five.

He started back towards the house. As he crested a hill that formed one side of the valley that sheltered the house, he became aware of a heady, familiar scent – it made him drop to a crouch. Wolfbloods, and not any he recognised. Down on the road he saw three figures – two men and a woman. Their scent was tinged, the same way that city Wolfblood's was. They came from the same place as Dacia, and he didn't trust them, either.

He ran for the house as fast as his human form could carry him. Bursting in the front door, he found everyone in the kitchen.

'Wolfbloods!' Aran shouted. 'Wearing black – coming this way!'

'I – I can tell them he's already gone,' said Dacia. Now she'd heard Gerwyn's side of the story she didn't know what to believe, but if Sweeney got to him they'd never find out the truth.

'There's no point,' said Gerwyn. He made for the door. 'I should never have put you in this situation. I'm off.'

'Dad, wait,' said Rhydian, following. 'They're too close and–'

'Hello?' said an unexpected voice. 'Anyone home?'

The room fell silent. Aran backed away as a man entered the room. It wasn't one of the Wolfbloods he'd just seen. This was a small human with a grey beard and damp trousers. He was wearing the sort of helmet that Aran had seen human cubs wear when they rode the two-wheeled things they called bicycles.

'Um,' said the man awkwardly. 'Sorry. Door was open.'

'Hello, Mr Jeffries,' said Jana.

'Jana!' said Mr Jeffries. 'So, the rumours are true – I was at the Kafe and Liam told me that you were up here. Welcome back to Stoneybridge!'

'Our travellers' camp got raided,' Jana told him. 'We lost our home.'

'That's terrible. I'm so sorry. I came to have a chat about your education while you're here, Jana. You're always welcome to come back to Bradlington High.'

'Er – have a seat, Mr Jeffries,' said Rhydian, waving at the table and pushing Gerwyn towards it too. He whispered in Gerwyn's ear as he passed. 'Keep him here, it'll buy us time.'

Jeffries noticed Dacia. 'Hi,' he said, 'weren't you at the Careers Fair?'

'Yes – I . . . was just saying what a great event it was.'

'She's got to go now though,' Rhydian interrupted. 'She's meeting a friend.'

Aran followed Rhydian and Dacia out. He'd always rather leave a room whenever a human entered it. Outside, a brisk wind was slicing its way around the house.

Rhydian caught his arm. 'I've got an idea,' he whispered in Aran's ear.

The three Segolia employees stood on the hill. The woman – Victoria Sweeney, Rhydian assumed – was flanked by two bruiser types that looked as if they belonged outside the door of a nightclub.

'Hello, Rhydian,' she said, as he and Dacia made their way over. 'Are you going to hand your father over or do we have to come in there and get him?'

'Might be a bit risky,' he pointed out, 'with our human teacher inside.'

'He won't be in there forever.'

'What happens if I do hand him over?' Rhydian asked. 'He's innocent.'

'That's for others to decide.'

'And if they decide he's guilty?'

Victoria Sweeney smiled, but it wasn't friendly. 'He gets his just punishment. We take him far away, where the cold north wind blows and wolves roam wild. Then we leave him there.'

The way she said it put ice into Rhydian's heart. 'That's not justice!'

She snarled then, baring her teeth and letting her wolf surge up into her eyes so fast that it took Rhydian by surprise. She looked dangerous. Terrifying. 'It's Wolfblood justice,' she hissed.

Rhydian swallowed, his heart hammering. 'Give me fifteen minutes, OK? Let me talk to him.'

He left Dacia there and returned to the house. Jeffries was just leaving as Rhydian came in the back to find his dad kneeling in front of his mum.

'This could be the end for me, Ceri,' said Gerwyn. 'I don't expect you to love me – or like me. Just a little forgiveness, that's all I'm asking . . .'

'Sorry, Dad,' Rhydian said. 'But for all our sakes, I'm going to have to throw you to the wolves . . .'

He pulled them all into a huddle and told them his plan. It was desperate, but it might just work.

'All right,' said Gerwyn. 'Let's go.'

Rhydian led the way; Sweeney and her cronies were

already making their way down the hill. 'He's coming,' he called out.

Gerwyn walked beside Rhydian until they got to the bottom of the hill. Then he stopped dead, as if he'd lost his nerve. 'Rhyd,' he said, deliberately speaking just loud enough for Sweeney and her men to hear. 'I'm sorry – I can't do this.'

Gerwyn took off at a flat run, heading for the forest. Rhydian watched as Sweeney and her goons chased after him at full pelt.

Gerwyn weaved and dodged through the trees. Then he doubled back, crossing behind Sweeney and her men. It was enough to lose them, if only for a few moments. He stopped, catching his breath.

'Gerwyn!' hissed a voice. Gerwyn spun, and saw Aran appearing out of the ground from the tunnel Rhydian had told him about. Gerwyn laughed, more relieved than he had ever been in his life. He tore off his coat, hat and scarf and thrust them at the wild Wolfblood. 'Thank you,' he gasped.

'Go!' Aran told him, pulling on Gerwyn's clothes over his own.

Gerwyn dropped into the tunnel, his wolf eyesight enough to show him the way. Rhydian, Ceri and Jana were waiting for him in the den, and he couldn't help whooping with relief as he found himself back in the house.

'Rhydian!' he laughed, pulling his son into a fierce hug. 'That was pure genius!'

'How did you lose them?' Ceri asked, as if she couldn't believe he'd managed it.

Gerwyn puffed out his chest. 'I've a few moves Victoria Sweeney doesn't know about. I can still do Eolas – she can't! None of them city Wolfbloods can.'

'So the switch went OK?' asked Jana.

'Oh yes,' Gerwyn laughed. 'Like clockwork. Aran will lead them a merry dance.'

Jana smiled. 'He couldn't wait to get back to the pack, anyway. He won't stop for anything until he finds them. Sweeney will have to give up long before that.'

Rhydian grinned. 'Come on, Dad. I'll show you the room you can use.'

Gerwyn's happiness faded. 'Son,' he said. 'You've bought me some time, that's all. I have to use it to get away.'

'You're leaving?' Rhydian said, in disbelief. 'Again?'

'Someone at Segolia's covering their tracks. They may have gone for now but trust me – they'll be back. I can't put you in any more danger. When things die down, I'll come and find you. OK?'

Later, Rhydian watched as his mum granted his dad the rite of Enouwian. Gerwyn hadn't even had to ask her, in the end – she'd offered. Rhydian had an idea that Ceri still had a soft spot for Gerwyn, really.

'I grant thee Enouwian,' Ceri said quietly, after placing a wreath of herbs on Gerwyn's head as he knelt before her. 'With this rite our past wrongs are cleansed.'

'Sop wesan,' said Jana, watching over them.

'Sop wesan,' Ceri and Gerwyn repeated, in unison.

Yes, thought Rhydian, smiling sadly as his mum kissed his dad on the head. *Yes. May it be true.*

Nine

The Kafe was buzzing, but Katrina was nowhere to be seen. Kay and Kara, more than a bit tired of doing most of the work, were trying to shoo the stubborn customers out. It was closing time, after all.

'The same goes for you two,' Kara told Tom and Shannon, who sat at a table surrounded by wrapping paper and Sellotape. 'Whose birthday is it, anyway?'

'They're going away presents for Jana and her mum,' Tom explained. 'They're leaving tomorrow.'

There was a commotion and Katrina clattered down the stairs carrying an old cardboard box. 'Look what I found in the attic!' she said excitedly. 'Bernie's old toy box!'

The other two Ks gathered around. They weren't much interested in the toy cars and notebooks, but right at the bottom were a few items that really caught their attention.

'Is this . . . bone?' Katrina asked, pulling out a large horn-shaped object covered with intricate carvings. 'Ew!'

'I think this is too,' said Kay, finding a small white

disc like the pendant from a necklace. She held it up for a closer look. 'It's got a dog on it.'

Tom and Shannon glanced at each other. A *dog*? They went over to look.

'Here's the good stuff!' Kara picked up a small gold brooch and a tiny carved ring. 'These have both got dogs on them too. Are they medieval, or something?'

'I think they could be older,' Shannon said. She knew she and Tom were both thinking the same thing. Those weren't dogs – they were wolves. She grabbed her phone and started taking photos.

'So are they valuable, then?' Katrina asked. 'Bernie obviously didn't think so – we asked him if we should send anything we found up there to him and he said we could just dump it.'

'Could be worth a fortune,' said Kara. 'Well, not the bits of bone, but these jewels and accessories.'

'Think of what we could buy if we sold it all!' Katrina crowed.

'Look,' said Shannon. 'We don't know if any of it's genuine yet. You need to take these to someone who knows their history.'

'Jeffries!' Kay and Kara said, together.

Kara grabbed the ring and tried to put it on her finger, but it was too small. Katrina tried too, but it didn't fit her either. When Kay tried, though, it slipped straight on. The only problem was, she couldn't get it off again.

'It's stuck,' she said.

Kay pulled at it one more time and the ring shot off her finger and fell to the floor, snapping in two.

'Kay!' Katrina snapped. 'You've ruined it! Get out!'

Kay, upset, grabbed her bag and left. The rest of them – Shannon included – were more interested in retrieving the broken ring, but Tom was worried about Kay. He followed her out and found her crying under the stone archway that led out of Stoneybridge's main square.

He pulled a packet of tissues out of his pocket and handed them to her. 'Here,' he said. 'They didn't mean it.'

Kay shrugged. 'I don't care if they did or not. I'm sick of this place. Katrina's all about the Kafe, Kara's talking uni. Where does that leave me?'

Tom knew what she meant. Shannon was excited by the idea of life after school – starting out on her career. Rhydian spent most of his time with Jana and Ceri. Sometimes Tom felt as if they had forgotten he existed. 'Yeah,' he said softly.

'Sorry,' Kay said. 'Dumping all this on you.'

'It's all right,' Tom said. 'You coming back inside?'

'Nah, I think I'll go home. See you later.'

Tom watched Kay disappear into the dark. *Funny how people surprise you sometimes*, he thought. He'd always thought she was pretty, but maybe underneath it all Kay was nice too.

'Come on,' Shannon called, coming out of the Kafe with an armful of presents. 'We'll be late for the party!'

They needn't have hurried. The party fizzled out as soon as Shannon showed Ceri and Jana the bone pieces Katrina had let her take from Bernie's box.

'There was jewellery too,' Shannon explained, handing over the bone horn and small carved disc. 'It all looked really old.'

Ceri examined the carvings on the horn. 'This is ágenspraec. An old Wolfblood language. The inscription is a memorial to an alpha killed in battle with a human tribe, the Saesons.'

'The . . . Saxons?' Shannon suggested.

Rhydian raised his eyebrows. 'From the Dark Ages?'

Ceri looked up. 'Dark? That was our time. Wolfblood kingdoms were rich and powerful. Only the strong survived – and our tribes were the strongest of all.'

Shannon shook her head in amazement. 'People called the Vikings "the wolves of the North". Maybe they actually were! And look, there's more . . .' She showed Jana and Ceri the pictures she'd taken of the other items.

'Who has these?' Jana asked.

'Katrina – she's taking them in to show Jeffries,' Shannon told her.

'She can't do that,' said Jana firmly. 'They're ours. We're not leaving until we get them back.'

'You can't just steal them,' Shannon exclaimed, horrified.

'It's our history!'

'It's everyone's history!' Shannon insisted. 'These belong in a museum.'

Jana looked disgusted. 'Locked in a glass case? It's not just the past to us, Shannon. I'm not leaving Stoneybridge without those finds!' She grabbed the two artefacts and stormed up the stairs.

Ceri looked apologetic. 'Perhaps you had better go,' she told Tom and Shannon, before heading after Jana.

'Sorry,' said Rhydian.

'You're not going to let her do this, are you?' Shannon asked him. 'If she gets caught breaking into the Kafe . . .'

'No one's breaking in anywhere,' Rhydian said. 'I'll deal with Jana.'

Tom grabbed a handful of crisps from one of the sorry-looking snack bowls. 'Well,' he sighed. 'I've been to better parties . . .'

Mr Jeffries was extremely excited by the box and its contents. 'We'll need an expert opinion,' he said to the class in form time the next morning, 'but these look very much to me like genuine Saxon or Viking jewellery. What really fascinates me is this wolf . . . Katrina, why don't you leave them with me?' Jeffries suggested. 'I'd like to do some research. We'll pick this up in history this afternoon.'

For a moment it looked as if Katrina might argue, but then she muttered, 'OK.'

'It's a pity we don't know where they came from,' the teacher added. 'Communities would often bury their valuables just before a battle – and unfortunately they often wouldn't live to dig them back up . . .'

'Wait,' said Rhydian. 'Are you saying there could be more out there?'

The idea went around the class like wildfire. More treasure, waiting to be found . . . But right then the bell rang. The first class of the day was PE with Miss Graham, who had a thing for making them all do cross-country running.

Rhydian was perfectly happy to run as far and as often as the teacher wanted. This time Jimi was, in fact, winning against Rhydian – or at least, he thought he was. Rhydian drew him out a bit and made him work for it, but, once they were clear of the grounds and along the forest road, he pulled up.

'Ha-ha!' Jimi laughed triumphantly, as he sailed past. 'Loser!'

Tom slowed, puzzled, but Rhydian waved him on. 'I'm fine,' he gasped. 'Stitch!' Rhydian waited until the rest of the class had passed him and then straightened up. A second later, he dashed off into the woods.

Ten

Rhydian made quick work of doubling back towards the school. He reached the fence beyond the school field and checked to see that there was no one around before leaping over it in one jump. Slipping back into the building, Rhydian listened outside Mr Jeffries' classroom, relieved to hear him in full-on teaching mode. He wasn't coming out any time soon.

Going into Jeffries' office, Rhydian quietly locked the door behind him. There was no sign of Katrina's box on the desk. On the wall behind the desk hung a picture of Mr Jeffries himself, which every self-respecting student of Bradlington High knew hid a 'secret' safe. Rhydian moved the picture out of the way. He put his ear to the dial and began to turn it, listening for the tell-tale 'clunk' that would signify that the tumblers inside had dropped into place. He was almost there, his ear still pressed against the dial, when someone rattled the handle to Jeffries' door.

'Rhydian,' hissed Shannon's voice from the other side of the opaque glass, 'I know you're in there!'

Rhydian ignored her, still trying to open the safe.

'Rhydian!' she said, more loudly this time, and then, even louder, '*Rhydian!*'

He opened the door, pulling his friend inside. 'Sssh!'

'I knew you were up to something!' Shannon said, crossing her arms.

'It's Wolfblood history, OK?' Rhydian told her. 'It all belongs with the wild pack!' He went back to the safe, still determined to unlock it.

'Britain's history is important too,' Shannon insisted. 'And if the secret comes out one day, maybe proving that your history is *our* history might help.'

There was a knock at the door. 'Mr Jeffries?'

They both froze, staring at each other. It was Miss Graham, the PE teacher! She must have realised they'd both ducked out of class. Rhydian shut the safe door and put the painting back just before she walked in.

Miss Graham raised her eyebrows at them. 'Little lost, aren't you?'

Their trespassing earned them both a lunchtime detention with Miss Graham, who favoured running laps instead of essays. *Still,* Shannon reflected, as she puffed unhappily after a perfectly composed Rhydian, *at least I stopped the Wolfblood artefacts from disappearing. For now, anyway.*

'You don't understand,' said Rhydian. 'Jana's having a tough time getting the pack to accept her as leader. If she

78

returns with those Wolfblood artefacts they'll take it as a sign that she's connected to their ways of old.'

Shannon sighed. She still didn't agree, but she could see Rhydian's point.

Later, the problem became even more pressing, as Jeffries announced that Kara and Katrina had found Bernie's old diary. It had been in the same box as the artefacts, and recorded exactly where they had been found. The Witch's Finger.

'We don't know much about this tribe,' the teacher said, 'but according to local legend, there were ghost warriors with glowing eyes keeping watch over their treasure. We could be on the verge of some real discoveries. But there's only one way to find out whether there's more artefacts to be found up there . . . So, who wants to come and survey the site with me early tomorrow morning?'

A forest of hands shot up. Little did Jeffries know that privately, three separate groups of his pupils – Katrina and Kara; Jimi, Liam and Sam; and Shannon – planned to go up to the Witch's Finger that very night.

The only two pupils not interested were Tom and Kay.

'Actually, we're going on a date,' Tom said, when Shannon found them in the darkroom, looking at some of Tom's pictures.

'Oh,' Shannon said, smiling, even though she suddenly didn't feel happy. 'Well . . . have a good time.' She left them to it. She'd just have to go up to the Witch's Finger on her own. She couldn't ask Rhydian. All he wanted to do was steal the artefacts for Jana.

But Rhydian had a plan all of his own anyway.

'Did you get them?' Jana asked, as soon as he arrived at the house after school.

'No. Sorry,' he said. 'But there could be a lot more. Follow me . . .'

The Witch's Finger stood in a hollow deep in the forest that surrounded Stoneybridge, a tall, narrow spire of stone that had been there for centuries. That night, the hollow was full of a thin, cold, lingering mist that crept into the bones and swallowed anyone who walked into it. As Liam and Sam made their way down the slope, the haunting sound of a crow squawking echoed out of the trees.

Liam didn't like it. 'It's really cold down here,' he muttered, once they reached the bottom. 'Like, *weird* cold.'

There were sounds too. It wasn't just birds – there was something else. A whispering among the trees that seemed to be growing louder, as if there were unseen people hiding, watching them.

'Yeah,' agreed Sam. 'I don't like this . . .'

'You don't think the legend could be true, do you?'

Liam asked, as the two boys stood back to back, trying to peer through the mist.

'There's no such thing as ghost warriors,' said Sam unconvincingly. Another sound echoed close to them, and he jumped. 'What was that?'

Jimi chose that moment to appear out of the mist, laughing fit to crack his cheeks. 'You pair of planks,' he hooted. 'Oh, your faces . . .'

'Ha ha,' said Liam, not at all impressed. 'Now – where do we dig?'

'Nowhere!' shouted a voice, as someone came running down the slope. It was Shannon. 'You are not digging up that treasure!'

'Oh great,' Jimi groaned. 'Little Miss History Swot is here.'

There was another commotion from above and suddenly Kara and Katrina rolled down the slope to land in a heap at the boys' feet.

'I hate this place!' said Katrina, struggling up.

'Well, push off, then!' said Jimi. 'We were here first.'

'No, you push off!' said Kara. 'Katrina found the accessories, so the treasure's ours!'

'What treasure?' Shannon shouted. 'You don't even know where to look! This isn't a prize in a raffle!'

The piercing, haunting sound of a hunting horn cut through the night. It called again, moving closer through the forest.

'It's . . . the ghost warriors!' Katrina cried.

Then out of the mist came three cowled figures, voices echoing as they repeated a series of strange words. Katrina screamed and ran, with Liam and Jimi hot on her heels.

'There's no such thing as ghosts,' Kara said firmly, though her voice was shaking as the figures moved closer. Suddenly, one of the cowled figures growled. There was a glimpse of a face under the hood – yellow eyes, bared teeth . . .

Kara screamed and ran, Sam with her all the way. Only Shannon was left . . .

. . . and she started to laugh.

Jana appeared. She was in human form. 'I had no idea the Ks could run so fast!' she said, laughing as Ceri and Rhydian joined her, also wearing cloaks.

'You all right?' Rhydian asked Shannon.

'Course. Why wouldn't I be?'

Jana sighed. 'I suppose you've come to stop us?'

Shannon shook her head. 'I'd rather you found this treasure than them. At least you respect its meaning. The question is, where is it?'

Ceri stepped forward, holding the carved bone disc between her palms. The rest of them fell silent as she spoke the words of a solemn incantation.

'We come to honour the memory of our ancestors,' Ceri said, in the Wolfblood language. 'To bring their lives into the light again. Show us the way.'

The bone disc shot out of her hand and flew across the hollow, embedding itself in the ground.

Ceri smiled. 'There,' she said. 'That is where we dig.'

Later, they all sat around the kitchen table in the Smiths' house, marvelling at what they had found. Everything had been inside a perfectly preserved clay pot – brooches, combs, necklaces – beautiful things that had lain unseen for centuries.

'This is the Battle of Badon Hill,' Ceri said, reading the inscription on a comb. 'I don't know what human history says, but our tribes fought together on this day – human and Wolfblood side by side.'

Jana was looking at the engravings on a cup. 'I know this story!' she realised, in wonder. 'It's Faolan and the Enchanted Wood! My father told it to me.'

Ceri passed the comb to Rhydian and picked up a necklace made of bone discs. It had a piece missing, and she retrieved the carved wolf-head disc that had shown them where the hoard lay buried. 'Now I understand its power,' she murmured, fitting the two together and putting the complete necklace over Jana's head. 'This is the traditional emblem of a pack leader. You should wear it on our return.'

Jana's smile suddenly turned into anxiety as she caught a scent from outside. Rhydian and Ceri smelled it too.

'What is it?' Shannon asked.

'Aran,' said Jana, standing up. 'It's Aran . . .'

They went outside to see Aran stumbling into the yard. He was exhausted and dirty, almost dropping to his knees.

'They've gone,' he said, broken-hearted. 'The pack – I searched the whole territory. Nothing, not even a scent.'

Ceri growled. 'Meinir,' she said. 'We left her with the pack for too long. She's taken over.'

Jana, stunned, took off the necklace. She held it out to Ceri. 'Put it with the rest.'

'It is yours,' Ceri told her, but Jana shook her head.

'I'm not pack leader any more,' she said, her eyes filling with tears.

Eleven

The moon would be full tonight. Jana stared at herself in the mirror, feeling different somehow. She'd heard Ceri and Rhydian talking about her the night before. They had been whispering, as if they somehow thought that not being an alpha any more meant she'd lost all her wolf senses too and wouldn't hear them. They thought she was marwol. Maybe they were right. Jana didn't care.

The house seemed empty without Aran. As much as he'd disliked being indoors, he'd helped to fill this place. But he'd gone, slipping out into the night even though she had asked him to stay.

'Meinir's betrayal has tainted me,' he'd said. 'I must find my sister and call her to account for her crimes. No matter what, you will always be my alpha, Jana.'

Jana wondered how that could be true when she had no pack. Even her father had rejected her.

In the kitchen she found find Ceri trying to work the washing machine. She looked up as Jana appeared, frowning to see her in her school uniform. 'What are you doing, cariad?' she asked.

Jana shrugged off the endearment. 'Going to school.'

Ceri looked uncertain. 'On full moon?'

'Why not? Rhydian's going, isn't he?'

'Meinir took your pack,' Ceri reminded her softly. 'A Wolfblood cannot just bury that kind of pain. Listen to me, sweetheart . . .'

'Stop calling me that!' Jana shouted. 'You're not my mother. I'm your alpha!'

'I've been abandoned too,' Ceri reminded her. 'If you cannot stay home for your own sake, then stay for mine. Please.'

Jana knew Ceri was right. They needed each other, now more than ever. But a wave of anger surged up through her, washing away Jana's sympathy. She was supposed to be an alpha! She glanced down at the table and the bold red print of another final demand from the electricity company. Snatching it up, she waved it at Ceri.

'You want to stay? Get a job. If not – leave, like the rest!' She stormed out.

The class was all gathered in the assembly hall, watching as the local museum presented Mr Jeffries with a cheque to say thank you for the donation of the artefacts that had recently been found in the area. Shannon was on the stage along with Katrina and Kay, posing as a photographer took a picture for the local paper.

'If we hadn't gone out on our date, that'd be our picture in the paper,' Kay told Tom, as they sat together in the audience.

'If your picture was in the paper no one'd be looking at the treasure, would they?' Tom said, rewarded for his smooth talking when Kay snuggled into his shoulder. This having a girlfriend thing was nice.

Rhydian saw Jana walk in just as Jeffries was holding up the ancient alpha necklace. For a second he thought she was going to go for him. Rhydian got up and blocked her way, staring her down.

'*What?*' she asked, baring her teeth. Rhydian saw with shock that her eyes were yellowing. He grabbed her in a hug as applause broke out and Jeffries declared that the assembly was over. Jana dragged herself free and Rhydian had just enough time to see that her face was back to normal before she barged her way out of the hall with the rest of the Bradlington High students.

Kay saw Tom watching Rhydian and Jana. 'Do you fancy her, or something?' she asked.

'What?' Tom asked, shocked. 'No!' Still, he got up and left her there, running after Rhydian with Shannon.

'I thought she was going to stay at home?' Shannon said to Rhydian in the corridor.

'So did I,' Rhydian said, frowning. 'The pull of the moon's too strong for her this month. Her scent's changed. She's got the marwol in her.'

'The what?' asked Shannon.

Rhydian sighed. Trying to explain Wolfblood ways to humans was so difficult. 'When a Wolfblood is really hurting, they *change* on a full moon. This is where you get your horror stories about werewolves. She's still Jana, but it's the marwol too. She doesn't know the difference. We need to get her out of school and into the den.'

They caught up with Jana in the form room.

'Jana, please,' Rhydian said. 'Tell Jeffries you're ill, and go home.'

'You can't tell me what to do,' she said, crossing her arms.

'We're your friends,' Tom reminded her. 'Your pack.'

Jana shook her head dismissively. 'I'm not your alpha. Your fear's not my problem. And I'm done pretending I'm something I'm not.'

It was in art class that things went really wrong. Jimi started teasing Katrina – she was trying to paint a picture of her poodle, Tallulah Pallulah. Katrina loved her pet, but it was so badly behaved that her mum was threatening to get rid of her.

'No wonder your mother's giving the dog away,' Jimi said, sniggering at her attempt. 'Is it some sort of mongrel? Or just a genetic mutation?'

'Get lost,' said Katrina, trying not to cry.

'If it was here I'd have it put down,' Jimi added, laughing.

Before he even knew what was happening, Jana had attacked, grabbing Jimi's canvas and smashing it hard over his head so that it hung around his neck like a collar. The class gasped as Jana grabbed Jimi's brush and dunked it in a pot of red paint before daubing it all over his face.

'What are you doing?' Jimi cried 'Get off me!'

Rhydian got to her before the teacher did, trying to drag her away. 'Jana, stop it!'

She struggled, kicking and snarling. Jimi stood in the middle of the classroom, humiliated as they all laughed at him.

'You've hardly been back three days and I'm already contemplating suspension,' Jeffries said angrily, once he had Jana in his office. 'You're in detention every single night, until I'm satisfied that–'

The door burst open and Kara and Katrina came dashing in.

'Don't come in without knocking!' Jeffries shouted, close to losing his rag completely.

'Sorry, sir – but we thought you should hear the full

story,' said Kara. 'Jimi's been bullying Katrina. Jana was just sticking up for the underdog. We think Jimi should get punished, not Jana.'

Jeffries crossed his arms. 'Well, I applaud your loyalty to a fellow pupil . . . and in return for supporting her, you can both have the honour of joining her in detention tonight.'

'For what?' Kara asked indignantly.

'For barging in without knocking! Jimi will be joining you too. Now get out, all of you. And, Jana – for the last time, sort out your work experience! You're running out of time.'

'Already sorted, sir,' Katrina piped up quickly. 'She's doing it at the Kafe.'

'You didn't have to do that,' Jana told the two girls, once they were out of Jeffries' office.

'You didn't have to stick up for Tallulah Pallulah.' Katrina still looked tearful. 'I can't even defend my own dog!'

Jana sighed, exasperated. 'If she's your dog, then just tell your mum you're not letting her go.'

'But she's in charge,' Katrina protested, 'and Dad won't have Tallulah in the house any more.'

'You're being pathetic!' Jana told her. 'Come on . . .'
She dragged them both into the girls' toilets and

demanded to see what make-up they had with them. Katrina and Kara were confused and nervous. This wasn't the slightly weird Jana they were used to – this girl was different.

Jana rooted through their make-up bags and pulled out various things before giving them both a makeover there and then. Strong eyeliner with killer flicks, red lipstick . . .

Katrina looked at herself in the mirror. 'It's a bit . . .'

'Scary,' Kara finished for her, and then added quickly, so as not to upset Jana, 'In a good way!'

'Scary's good,' Jana told them. 'People don't mess with you.'

Shannon came in. Jana stared at her. 'What are you looking at?'

'N-nothing,' Shannon said quietly. 'I just wanted to see you.'

Jana turned her back. 'Well, I'm busy.'

Kay came in as Shannon left. 'You get around,' Kay said, looking at Jana harshly.

'Leave her alone, Kay,' said Kara. 'She stood up for Katrina – you didn't.'

Kay crossed her arms. 'She's after my boyfriend!'

'Er, no,' said Jana. 'I'm not. If you don't trust Tom, that's your problem.'

Jana finished her own make-up and marched out of

the bathroom as if she owned the whole school, Katrina and Kara close behind her.

'Maybe that's what all this is about,' Shannon muttered to Tom, as they watched the three girls stalk down the corridor. 'Finding a new pack to lead.'

Twelve

Kay came up to Jana again over lunch. 'I just wanted to say sorry, for earlier,' she said, before looking over at Kara and Katrina. 'And to you guys, for not being there.'

'Go away,' Jana snarled.

'Chill out, Jana,' Kara said, shooting her a dirty look. 'You're not in charge. Kay, sit here – guess where I'm going for work experience? Segolia! It was Jana's idea.'

The Ks squealed with excitement. 'Jana's going to work in the Kafe, with you, Tom and Rhydian,' Katrina added.

'What?' Kay said, disgusted. 'I'm not working at the Kafe if *she*'s there.'

Tom, Shannon and Rhydian walked into the canteen just as Jana stood, picking up her tray and spaghetti bolognese. 'Well,' she shouted at the Ks, 'I wouldn't spend a day serving dirt like this to people like *you*!'

Tom put one hand on her arm. 'Jana,' he said. 'It's cool. Just chill, yeah?'

Kay looked up at him, incredulous that her boyfriend had waded in to help this girl *again*. 'Don't defend her!'

93

'No wonder you're all pathetic,' Jana went on. 'You're pumped full of this! Hey – you!' she yelled at Mrs Harries, the dinner lady, as she marched up to the serving hatch. 'I wouldn't feed this to a *dog*! We want real meat, not this slime!'

Kay tried to drag Tom away, but he was staring at Jana in horror. So was everyone else – Rhydian, Shannon, Kay, the rest of the class, Mr Jeffries. They were all looking at her as if she was a complete and utter freak.

Jana picked up her plate and flung it straight at Kay, who screamed as the food splattered all over her.

Then Jana ran.

Ceri had decided to see if Katrina's mum, Karen, would give her a job at the Kafe. She saw Karen coming across the cobbles of Stoneybridge square, struggling to control a large white poodle. Someone had seen fit to dye the poor creature's ears and tail a bright, fluorescent pink. *No wonder it's trying to get away*, thought Ceri.

'Hello,' she said, sticking out one hand for Karen to shake. 'I'm Ceri. My daughter's in school with your daughter . . .' Ceri took a deep breath and reeled off her sales pitch before she could lose her nerve. 'I am well travelled, self-sufficient, with diverse experience of . . .' a scent suddenly wafted to her '. . . rabbits!'

Tallulah Pallulah chose that moment to jump up at her. Ceri, taken by surprise, snarled. The terrified dog put its silly pink tail between its legs and bolted.

'Oh no!' Karen groaned, watching the poodle disappear into the distance. 'Katrina's going to *kill* me!'

'I can get her,' Ceri said, and ran after the dog before Karen could stop her.

Rhydian chased Jana into the woods. With her wolf speed, she was quick, but he was still quicker. He tackled her to the ground, leaping as if he were in wolf form and dragging her down, holding on to her until she stopped fighting.

'Jana, Jana,' he said. 'Calm down . . . it's all right . . .'

'It's not all right,' Jana said, against his chest, sobbing. 'What's happening to me? You were right, I can't control it.'

'It's only this full moon, because of what happened with the pack.'

'This isn't me,' Jana said. 'It's like another wolf's taken over. Am I evil?'

'No. Just in pain.'

Jana sighed. 'Lock me in the den tonight. Promise me?'

Rhydian nodded. 'I promise.'

Ceri appeared with Tallulah Pallulah at her heels. She

smiled sadly at Jana as she and Rhydian stood up. 'I tried to get a job,' she said. 'But I didn't.'

'I'm sorry, Ceri,' said Jana, hugging her. 'I owe you everything.'

They went back to Stoneybridge, deciding on the story they were going to tell Jeffries as they went. Tallulah Pallulah followed Ceri happily, as if they had been best friends all their lives.

Karen was gobsmacked when she saw how well behaved Katrina's dog was being. 'Why didn't you say you were a dog trainer?' She knelt to pet the poodle. 'What are your rates?'

Jana and Rhydian laughed. It looked as if Ceri had got herself a job after all.

Rhydian and Jana smoothed things over with Jeffries. They told him that Jana was upset because Gerwyn had run off and stolen all of Ceri's money. The teacher bought it, but told her she'd still have to do detention. That was fine by Jana. It meant she'd have time to say sorry to everyone she needed to apologise to. She found the three Ks and Jimi together when she went in to sit her detention after school. They all stopped talking.

'I owe you all an apology,' she said. 'I'm sorry for the trouble I caused.'

'Whatever.' Jimi shrugged.

'Water under the bridge,' Kara told her, with a sugary smile.

Jana frowned. She hadn't expected them to accept her apology so easily. 'By the way, Katrina, you can keep your dog.'

Katrina looked surprised. 'What?'

'My mum's training it,' Jana explained. 'She's as good as gold now. And look, I'm sorry for what I said. I'd love to work for you if you'll still have me.'

'Joining us for detention tonight, Kay?' Jeffries asked, bustling in with an armful of folders.

'No, sir. Just going,' Kay told him, leaving the room.

Detention was as boring as always, but it passed eventually. On the dot of six o'clock, Jeffries stood up and dismissed them. Jana was the first out of the door – there was still plenty of time before moonrise, but she didn't want to risk being caught outside when the change came. Not this time, not with the marwol still inside her.

'Jana,' Kara called, 'wait a sec!'

Jana turned as Kara and Jimi caught up with her, but Katrina had gone. 'Mrs Harries?' Kara said. 'The dinner lady? She's really upset.'

'I'll see her tomorrow,' Jana promised.

'But she's here now,' Kara told her. 'In the kitchen, cleaning up. She's always the last to leave.'

'She's been here years,' said Jimi. 'You owe it to her to apologise.'

Jana followed them to the canteen. The kitchen shutters were all down and bolted fast. Kay was standing by the kitchen door, looking in. Jana went to look too, moving into the open doorway. Jimi shoved her hard from behind and she stumbled forward. The door slammed behind her. Jana turned and threw herself against it, but heard the key turn in the lock. She was trapped.

'Let me out!' she screamed, as rage coursed through her and her eyes yellowed.

'Don't worry,' shouted Jimi. 'We won't leave you in there all night!'

'You don't know what you're doing!' Jana shouted, feeling the wolf beginning to gather in her veins. She couldn't be trapped here during a full moon!

'Oh, I think we do,' Jimi shouted back, as they left her there.

Tom and Shannon were waiting outside the Kafe with Tallulah Pallulah.

Katrina appeared, beaming from across the square as she saw her poodle. 'Tallulah Pallulah!' she cried, as her mum appeared out of the Kafe. 'Oh, look, she's being so well behaved! Did Jana's mum do this?'

Karen nodded. 'She's coming once a week to train her.'

'Katrina,' Tom said. 'You haven't seen Kay, have you? We were supposed to have a date but she hasn't showed up.'

Katrina gave Tom a guilty look and then told them everything. A few minutes later, Tom was pulling his phone out as Shannon was climbing on to her bike, both of them trying not to panic.

'I'll catch you up,' Tom told Shannon, as he dialled Rhydian's number.

Rhydian and Ceri ran for the school as soon as they heard. They reached Bradlington High just as Tom and Shannon were dumping their bikes. Rhydian looked down to see his hands beginning to vein – it was no good, the transformation was coming. He and Ceri couldn't help – they'd be seen.

'We're too late!' Ceri cried.

It was all down to Tom and Shannon now. 'Make sure she stays in there,' Rhydian told them. 'Remember – the wolf isn't Jana!'

Inside, Kay was beginning to feel uncomfortable. There were strange sounds coming from the locked kitchen. What if Jana was having a fit?

'Is she . . . growling?' Jimi asked, his ear to the door.

'Just open it,' Kay said, pushing him out of the way and moving to turn the key in the lock.

'Stop!' Tom shouted, as he and Shannon skidded into the canteen. 'We'll take it from here.' He grabbed the key from Kay.

'I'll stay with you,' Kay told him.

'You can't,' said Tom.

'Why not?' When Tom didn't say anything, Kay put her hands on her hips. 'You want to be alone with her, don't you?'

'No,' said Tom. He couldn't think of any other way to get her out of there, so he said, 'I just don't want to be alone with you.'

Kay looked as if he'd slapped her across the face. 'What?'

'We're done.'

'Why?' Kay asked, upset, as everyone else stared at them.

'Just . . . because, OK?' Tom shouted. She had to go, *now* and if this was the only way . . .

Kay ran out, her hands over her face. Jimi and Kara left too.

The snarling inside the kitchen was getting worse. Something threw itself against the door, making it rattle on its hinges. Shannon jumped back, terrified, but Tom went to open the door.

'Wait!' Shannon hissed. 'What are you doing? It's the marwol – you heard what Rhydian said!'

'That's Jana in there, Shan. You know it is,' said Tom. 'I'm not leaving her in there alone. She's scared. And maybe humans can do what Wolfbloods can't.'

He opened the door a crack, but couldn't see anything. Shannon grabbed his hand before he could go any further. 'Since when have you ever done anything stupid without me?' she said shakily.

Tom squeezed her hand. Together they stepped inside. Shadows danced around the kitchen, glancing off the clean chrome surfaces and gathering in corners. Tom and Shannon moved slowly, not letting each other go. They could feel the wolf there somewhere – breathing seemed to echo from everywhere at once – but they couldn't see it.

'Jana?' Tom called softly. 'It's all right. It's only us.'

Then, as suddenly as if she was made of shadows herself, wolf-Jana appeared, melting out of the darkness. She stood in front of them, yellow eyes gleaming.

'It's OK,' said Shannon. 'We're here for you.'

They both sank to one knee on the cold floor, bowing their heads. Being submissive, as if Jana was their alpha and not just their friend.

The sun rose next morning to find Rhydian and his mum running towards the school. They were exhausted now that the transformation had faded, but more than that, they were petrified of what they might find at Bradlington High. They reached the school before the sun was even properly up, ducking beneath the loose piece of fence that all the students knew about before dashing into the canteen and creeping towards the kitchen.

Everything was silent as Rhydian headed for the door. It was closed, but unlocked, and his heart pounded hard as he grasped the handle and glanced at Ceri. Together they took a deep breath, and pulled open the door.

There was just Jana, Tom and Shannon, all still dressed in the clothes they had been wearing the night before.

They were curled around each other, fast asleep.

Thirteen

It was supposed to be the first day of work experience, but Rhydian had no intention of going anywhere near the Kafe. He and his mum had decided it was more important to cheer Jana up. She was still upset after Aran's news about the pack and what had happened with the marwol. Ceri had come up with a great idea. All he had to do was pack his school bag with the tools she'd given him and . . .

A scent drifted to him through his open bedroom door. Ollie again! Rhydian whipped open the door, scaring his little foster brother so much that Ollie almost dropped what he was holding.

'Quit pratting about,' said Rhydian, grabbing the toy from Ollie's hand. It was a square metal box with a meter and flashing lights. 'What is this, anyway?'

'It's an EMF,' Ollie said, trying to grab it back. 'An electromagnetic field meter. Give it!'

Rhydian pushed past him and went downstairs, still holding the meter. 'Get ready for school!' he told Ollie, who made a face at his back.

Rhydian dumped the EMF meter on the kitchen table and stuck a slice of bread in the toaster. He spied Mrs Vaughan's mobile lying on the windowsill and deftly nabbed it.

'Morning,' he said nonchalantly.

'Possessed by any demons?' asked his foster mother.

Rhydian froze. What did she mean by that? He looked at her, scared of what he might see in her face, but Mrs Vaughan was smiling and nodding at Ollie's new toy. Rhydian sighed in relief – she was just teasing.

'One or two,' he said, turning away to make his toast and briefly wishing that it were more of the pizza Shannon had brought over for Jana to try the night before. Pizza made a great Wolfblood breakfast, especially if it had pepperoni on it . . . Not that Jana would agree. She hadn't even finished one slice. Rhydian sighed. He should have kept the bit she'd left instead of letting Shannon take it away from him, mother hen that she was. He found Jeffries' number and quickly sent a text: MORNING MR JEFFRIES. RHYDIAN IS SICK. FOOD POISONING. HAVE TO KEEP HIM HOME TODAY.

'Here's Jana,' Rhydian said, looking out of the window as Ollie appeared and retrieved his scanner. 'See you later!'

Rhydian went outside and took Jana's hand, leading her off towards the woods.

'Er – the Kafe is that way.' Jana pointed back down the road.

'We're not going to the Kafe,' he told her, grinning. 'Come on – this way!'

Neither of them saw Ollie watching them as he held his EMF meter, which was making a very strange sound.

Once they were far enough away from the house, Rhydian called Ceri and got her to phone Mr Jeffries. 'Tell him Jana's got food poisoning,' he said.

The last person Rhydian had to talk to was Tom. Unfortunately for him, with Rhydian and Jana bunking off, Tom was going to have to face a day in the Kafe alone with Kay and Katrina. Kay hadn't said a single word to him since he'd dumped her at full moon. Awkward.

'You're not coming, are you?' Tom asked dejectedly, when he phoned Rhydian to find out why they were late.

'Jana needs looking after. If anyone asks, we've got food poisoning, all right?' Rhydian told him. 'Shannon's at the pharmacy if you need rescuing.'

Tom shook his head, annoyed at being left on his own again. *As usual*, he thought. *Don't worry about Tom – just leave him to pick up the pieces*. 'Brilliant,' he said. 'I'll buy some plasters.' He hung up and then sent Shannon a text: R&J HAVE BUNKED OFF. MIGHT

FEED MYSELF THROUGH THE COFFEE GRINDER. HAVE FUN AT THE PHARMACY x

The thing was, though, that Shannon wasn't at the pharmacy. When she got Tom's text, she was standing right outside the Segolia building. She took a deep breath, and then headed for the main entrance.

The inside of the Segolia offices was as sharp and clean as a new pin. Shannon stood in reception and tried to calm her nerves as she waited for Dacia Turner. Even with everything that she'd discovered about her friends – about the world – in the past two years, this was the most excited she had ever been. This was a chance for her to see what it would be like to live her dream.

'I thought you dropped out?' said a familiar voice behind her.

Shannon raised her eyes to the heavens. *Great*, she thought. *The shine's already been knocked off the day*. She turned to see Kara, dressed in a peculiar see-through rain jacket and a shirt with the biggest bow the world had ever seen at her neck.

Dacia Turner appeared to take them both to the laboratories, which were so pristine and full of extraordinary scientific equipment that Shannon was overwhelmed.

'I believe you know Doctor Whitewood?' Dacia said

to the two girls, as they arrived as the scientist's desk. 'I'll leave you to it.'

'You work here?' Kara said, shocked, as Dacia walked away.

'Oh, you know,' shrugged the scientist, 'more science, fewer students. Well . . . usually. Kara – could you get a couple of Bunsen burners out of the cupboard for me? Over there . . .' She pointed to the far end of the lab.

Kara bustled off, evidently proud to have been given a task so quickly. Whitewood watched her go and then looked over at Shannon. 'Did you bring it?'

'Yeah.' Shannon pulled a plastic tub from her bag. In it was Jana's half-eaten slice of pizza from the night before. This was what they had asked Shannon for when they had called to offer her work experience at Segolia – a sample of wild Wolfblood DNA.

Whitewood took the box from her and removed the pizza, scraping a small sample from the bitten area. 'We'll get this sequenced and compare it to the tame samples.'

Shannon couldn't help but smile, despite the guilt – it was too exciting. Just think what this one slice of old pizza was going to tell them about an entire species!

Having Kara there made things awkward. Dr Whitewood had to make an excuse every time she wanted to talk to Shannon about the sample. It went into the sequencer straight away. When the results started to come in, Whitewood snatched a quick chance to show Shannon what she was seeing by tipping over a beaker and then sending Kara to sterilise the wet equipment.

'Take a look at this,' the scientist said quietly, indicating her screen.

Shannon ducked around the side of the bench to look at the computer screen. Two images were on it – different examples of DNA set up side by side for comparison.

Shannon knew what she was looking at, but not enough to be able to decipher all its secrets. 'Are they different, tame and wild?'

'I'll have a specialist take a look but . . . there are some discrepancies,' nodded Whitewood.

'So . . . why all this testing? What's Segolia looking for?'

Dr Whitewood hesitated. 'A cure.'

Shannon was shocked. 'For . . . for Wolfbloods?'

The scientist laughed, shaking her head. 'For humanity! One Wolfblood gene could be the key to the greatest medical breakthrough in history. The ability to rebuild cells, heal without medicine – all possible with Wolfblood DNA.'

Shannon was amazed. 'I can't believe you get to be a part of this,' she whispered. 'It's incredible!'

'Well, now you're a part of it too.'

Shannon took a deep breath. She'd hated lying to the others about what she was doing today – and despite the good it would do, she'd felt bad about sneaking Jana's DNA without asking.

'Your friends don't know you're here, do they?' Whitewood realised.

Shannon shook her head. 'I wanted to tell them, but . . . how can I? All this, they'll never see it as anything more than a threat.'

'Like I was?' asked Whitewood. 'I was wrong to pursue the Smiths the way I did. But Segolia's work thrives on openness, on sharing knowledge and ideas – human and Wolfblood. For mutual benefit. If they understood how important this work is, they might not be so quick to condemn you.'

Shannon bit her lip. 'You think I should tell them?'

Dr Whitewood smiled. 'Well,' she said, 'if you can keep their secret, I'm sure they can keep yours.'

Deep in the forest, Rhydian led Jana down into a gully, edged by huge walls of jutting sandstone that pointed up into the bright blue sky. As they moved closer, Jana saw caves in the rock. The rock was peppered with colourful scrawls of graffiti, written in English.

'Mum reckons it was a Wolfblood den, centuries ago,' Rhydian told her. 'She found it walking Katrina's dog.'

Jana pointed at the graffiti. 'But this is human.'

Rhydian put down his pack and leaned against a flat rock outside the biggest cave. 'Humans leave marks so everyone knows they were here.'

Jana nodded. She understood that. 'In the wild, whenever a pack moves on, they always leave a mark behind. We call it Beyanath. It's supposed to bless whichever new pack takes the place of the last. No one wants to be forgotten,' Jana echoed, her quiet voice sad.

'We won't be,' Rhydian told her, determined. He opened his backpack and showed her the tools inside. 'If this place was Wolfblood, it's our history too. It's time we left our own mark.'

Jana liked that idea. They were heading for the largest cave when Jana began to feel the first twinges of foreboding. It had been weighing on her since Rhydian had told her that Ceri thought this place was an ancient den. Something niggling, something not quite right . . .

'What is it?' Rhydian asked, sensing her worry.

'Ceri . . . never found a Beyanath, did she?'

'Here? She never mentioned it.' He headed for the cave mouth. 'Come on.'

The cave mouth was wide, but the light seemed to flee as soon as Jana stepped inside. Rhydian's footsteps echoed ahead, rolling around the space. His shadow flickered over the walls, as if there were a hundred ghosts rising out of the gloom.

Jana stopped, feeling something reaching out to her – not a thing but a feeling, so huge she couldn't ignore it. She was overwhelmed by a fear so potent she couldn't move. Sounds echoed out of the shadows – screaming. Terror. She pressed her hands over her ears, crying out as her veins began to blacken and her eyes yellowed.

'Jana?' Rhydian shouted, realising what was happening and running to her side. 'What is it?'

Jana screamed and ran out of the cave – straight into Rhydian's little brother Ollie.

'Argh!' Ollie yelled. 'Your eyes!'

Jana threw her hands up to her face, trying to calm herself enough to return to human form as Rhydian appeared behind her.

'Ollie, mate,' Rhydian said. 'It's all right, she's just – Ollie!' Rhydian shouted, but his brother, terrified, turned and ran.

'It was Ansion,' Jana said, gasping for breath as she recovered. 'They died in there, Rhydian. A whole pack, hunted on a full moon. That's why there was no Beyanath!'

Rhydian stared at her, shocked. 'But you weren't even using Ansion . . .' He looked in the direction that his little brother had run. 'I've got to get Ollie . . .'

Rhydian chased after his brother, following his scent trail and cursing himself. He should have known something like this was going to happen – especially after he'd caught him sneaking around this morning. His phone rang in his pocket and Rhydian paused, hoping it might be Ollie, but it wasn't – it was Tom.

'This isn't exactly a good time!' Rhydian told his friend.

'Mrs Vaughan is here, and she's looking for you,' Tom said. 'Ollie's missing.'

Rhydian shut his eyes. 'No, he's not – he's with me.'

There was a second's pause from Tom's end, and Rhydian realised that his foster mum must be standing right there. 'Then . . . bring him back?' Tom suggested tightly.

'Ollie saw Jana wolfing out. He's run off,' Rhydian hissed. 'Tell her . . . tell her Ollie called me and I'm taking him straight back to the Kafe, OK? Just . . . Just keep her there!' He rang off, leaving Tom to sort things out.

Ollie was quick and agile, but he was no match for Rhydian. The Wolfblood chased him down, cornering him at the edge of a cliff.

'Keep back!' Ollie shouted, backing away.

'Keep away from the edge,' Rhydian told him.

'Her eyes changed,' Ollie shouted. 'She looked right at me!' He held up the EMF meter. 'And this went crazy!

I'm not going anywhere until you tell me the truth.' Then he took another step backwards and disappeared over the cliff edge with a yell.

'Ollie!' Rhydian lunged for him, but he had gone.

'It's all right,' said a voice, from below. 'I used my superpowers to catch him.'

Rhydian looked down to see Jana, holding a very shocked Ollie. He was so relieved that he sat down, heavily, right there and then.

Fourteen

They went back to the cave entrance and sat on one of the stones to talk. Rhydian fiddled with the smashed bits of Ollie's EMF meter, but it was a goner for sure. He shivered to think that could easily have been Ollie, if not for Jana.

'Don't think we're going be able to glue this one back together, mate,' he said.

Ollie shrugged. 'Never really worked that well anyway.'

'What was it supposed to do?' Jana asked.

'Detect ghosts,' said Ollie, still subdued.

Jana laughed and then stopped when she saw the hurt look on Ollie's face. 'Sorry.'

'It's all right,' said Ollie. 'Maybe I'm just crazy.'

Jana sighed. 'You're not. I'm going to tell you something no one else knows except Rhydian. But you've got to keep it a secret, do you promise?'

'Jana . . .' warned Rhydian.

'It's all right,' said Ollie, curious and a bit excited. 'I promise.'

'I can see into the past,' Jana lied. 'When that happens,

my eyes go all . . . you know. Most of the time I can control it, decide when to use it, but this time I couldn't.'

Ollie stared at her with interest. 'Why not?'

'Because something terrible happened here. People were hunted, because . . . they were different.'

Ollie thought for a moment and then nodded. 'They want to be remembered.'

Jana stared at him. 'Ollie's right,' she said. 'If they're not remembered, this place is only ever going to be the place where they died. We should be making a memorial!'

The three of them worked on the carving together, choosing a large, flat rock that stood just outside the cave entrance. When they were done, they were all tired but happy, even Ollie.

Their good spirits died the minute they walked into the Kafe. Mrs Vaughan was sitting at a table in the corner – with Mr Jeffries. They stood up as they came in. Mrs Vaughan took Ollie home immediately, leaving Rhydian to the teacher's wrath.

'I don't know what you were doing,' said Jeffries, keeping his voice low and even, 'and frankly I don't care –'

'Sir,' Rhydian interrupted, 'this is my fault . . .'

Jeffries held up a hand. 'I don't want to hear it. Not

any more. You've had your fair share of warnings, so let me give you your last. One more misstep, and you're *both* out. Do you understand me?' He walked out without another word.

Rhydian looked over at Tom. 'Thanks for all your help, mate,' he said with a sarcasm that couldn't possibly be misunderstood.

Tom threw down the cloth he'd been holding. 'Oh no. You don't get to have a go at me – I've literally been cleaning up after you ALL DAY!'

Rhydian shook his head, disgusted. 'So you called Jeffries, then?'

'No!' said Tom angrily. 'But I wish I had!'

It was the end of the day and Shannon found herself on her own in the lab when the door opened and a tall man walked in. He was limping, badly, but still moved with the confidence of someone who knew exactly where they belonged. He headed right for Dr Whitewood's terminal and began to examine the samples they had been looking at earlier. Shannon wasn't sure what to say, so she kept quiet.

A few minutes later he gave a loud sigh. 'Oh, it's all so undramatic, isn't it? Given what it is you almost want it to glow or something, but DNA's DNA . . .' He smiled and stuck out his hand for her to shake.

'I'm Alexander Kincaid,' he said. 'This is my department.'

She shook his hand. 'Shannon Kelly . . . Work experience.'

Kincaid beamed at her. 'Oh, I know who you are. You brought us a wild Wolfblood DNA sample. You really are good, aren't you?'

Shannon blushed, embarrassed by such praise from a real scientist. But it got better. When Dacia came to collect Shannon and Kara to take them home, Whitewood and Kincaid both came down to the foyer to see them out. At the last minute, Kincaid stopped her.

'Shannon,' he said. 'I hope you know that what you've given us could change people's lives. Speaking of which . . . I want to be clear that if one day you decide to come and work for us – which I think you should – then whichever overpriced university hellhole you decide to go to . . . it's on us.'

Shannon felt her mouth drop open. Had he really just said that Segolia would pay her way through university?

'Just think about it,' said Kincaid, shaking her hand.

'I – I will . . .' said Shannon, dazed. 'Thank you.'

Dacia was quiet as she drove them back to Stoneybridge. Kara had asked to be dropped off at the Kafe, which worked for Shannon too. It was clear to her that she had to tell her friends what she'd done as soon as possible. The Kafe was where Tom would be and she had the vague idea that she wanted to tell him first.

But Shannon didn't have a chance to do anything the way she had planned. When they got to Stoneybridge, Dacia got out of the car too, clutching a file. She walked straight into the Kafe before Shannon had a chance to stop her.

Rhydian was behind the bar. His face darkened when he saw the city Wolfblood. 'What are *you* doing here?'

Dacia held out the file. 'You wanted answers. So did I,' she said, as Rhydian reluctantly took it from her. 'I'm so sorry, Rhydian. Gerwyn stole. Your dad was a fraud. He used you. It's all in there. I am your friend, Rhydian,' she added, 'whatever you might think.' And she disappeared out of the door again.

There was a moment of silence as Rhydian saw Shannon and realised what it meant. He stared at her with more anger than she'd ever seen from him. 'So you went to Segolia?'

'Look,' she began, 'it's not how you think . . .'

'Why did you lie?' Rhydian demanded.

'Because I knew you'd be unfair. The things they're doing . . . They want to pay my way through university!'

Rhydian uttered a harsh laugh. 'Glad someone's getting everything handed to them on a plate.'

'Hey,' she said, angry too now. 'I've never been handed anything. Why do you always go out of your way to misunderstand me?'

'Get out of my way,' Rhydian hissed, pushing past her. Jana followed him, which just left Tom. He stared at her as if he didn't know who she was, and Shannon felt her heart fracture, just a little.

Fifteen

Rhydian did not want to go to school. For a start, he didn't want to put up with another day of avoiding Shannon Kelly, especially not when she'd be crowing over her victory of getting Jeffries to set up an all-night session to watch the comet that would be passing over. Besides that, tonight was going to be a dark moon. That meant all Wolfbloods would be suffering. Already, his legs felt heavy and tired and he was getting a headache.

'Shannon knows it's the dark moon – she's done this deliberately,' he groused, as he and Jana headed through the forest.

'She's done it because it's the best night for star-gazing,' Jana corrected him.

'Now you're sounding like her.'

'No,' Jana said, exasperated, 'I'm sounding like someone who's already in enough trouble for bunking off work experience!'

They both stopped. Ceri was sitting on the old eagle statue that stood atop the hill, staring at the sky.

'Mum?' Rhydian asked. 'What are you doing?'

'Something's coming,' she said, in a strangely distant voice.

'Yeah,' said Jana. 'It's the comet.'

Ceri's eyes were dark and serious. 'Something bad will happen tonight. Very bad.'

Ceri couldn't tell them what this bad thing that was supposed to happen was, only that it was coming. Rhydian made her go home and they carried on into school – although by then, they were late.

'Ansion sees the past, Eolas the present,' Rhydian pointed out, as they wandered into the tent that had been set up in the playground. There were boards with star charts all over them. 'No one sees the future,' he added. 'Besides, we're not even Wolfbloods tonight.'

Tom stuck his head into the tent. 'Little help out here?' he said. 'Please?'

Shannon was overseeing the removal of some astronomy equipment from the back of a car. Rhydian and Shannon looked at each other and then Rhydian walked off. There was no way he was going to help her.

'When are you and Rhydian going to sort it out?' Jana asked Shannon.

'Tell him, not me!' Shannon exclaimed. 'All I've ever done is *not* do things for myself to help him. What's he done for me? Nothing. I have a life too, you know!'

'With Doctor Whitewood?' Jana asked. 'You know what she did.'

'And now she's changed,' said Shannon. 'Look – this is an amazing opportunity for me. Alex and Becca are doing brilliant things at Segolia, and I have a chance to be part of that. Where's the harm in helping to cure people?'

Jana was still doubtful. 'You really think they're OK?'

'Of course I do, otherwise Wolfbloods wouldn't work there and I wouldn't get involved. I'm not apologising.' She went off to sort something else out, and Jana went to talk to Tom.

'We have to end this feud,' she said.

'Yeah, but she does have a point,' said Tom. 'We stick our necks out for you Wolfbloods. All the time.'

'I know that. So does Rhydian.'

'Then why's he behaving like a total bin lid?'

Jana looked at him as if he were mad. 'He lost Maddy because of Whitewood. She works for Segolia. They're after his dad – and Shannon's going to join them. You work it out.'

A car pulled into the school grounds. Shannon recognised it with a smile. 'It's Becca!'

Rhydian couldn't believe it. What was Whitewood doing here? He started heading for her as the woman got out of the car, but Jana stopped him.

'Don't be stupid,' she hissed, as their science teacher, Miss Parish, greeted Dr Whitewood.

'It's so kind of you to do this for us,' Miss Parish was saying.

'It's my pleasure,' said Whitewood. 'Shannon's enthusiasm can be catching.' She opened the boot of her car. Inside was a telescope far larger than anything else set up in the school grounds. 'One telescope, courtesy of Mr Kincaid.'

'Wow,' said Shannon, in awe.

Miss Parish turned to Tom. 'Tom, give Doctor Whitewood a hand with this, would you? Shannon's cleared a space over here for it.'

'How are you, Tom?' asked the scientist, as they lifted the telescope into position.

'I'm OK,' Tom said and then glanced at Shannon before he added, 'No offence but this is a bit . . . unexpected.'

Whitewood looked at Shannon with raised eyebrows. 'You didn't tell them I was coming?'

Shannon looked awkward. 'The truth didn't work out so well last time I tried . . .'

Tom was getting pretty sick of his so-called friends shutting him out. 'Thanks for the trust, Shan,' he muttered.

The night wore on and the clouds broke up, revealing a clear, starlit sky. Rhydian's temper did not improve and

Jana only just managed to stop him smashing up the Segolia telescope when Whitewood left it unattended.

'You'll get expelled,' she warned him.

'I don't care,' Rhydian told her.

Jana was sick of his mood. 'Do it, then. Leave me and Tom to pick up the pieces. I lost my pack, Rhydian. You helped me get over it. Do the same for yourself instead of wrecking *this* pack. I know what Whitewood did, but things have changed. You need to move on. Like I did. Talk to Shannon.'

Rhydian wasn't keen, but he knew Jana was right. They'd already lost a pack each; he couldn't afford to lose the rest of this one. 'Fine,' he said, going over to Shannon. 'Shan . . .' he said, trying to catch her attention.

'Don't, Rhydian,' Shannon said, cutting him dead. She wasn't in the mood for another earful about how evil Segolia were.

'Shan,' Rhydian said, trying again.

'I said, don't!' Shannon said, hurrying away. Rhydian let her go, disgusted with himself for even bothering to try.

'What's going on?' Tom asked, appearing at his side.

'Forget it,' spat Rhydian, walking away. 'She can rot in Segolia the rest of her life if she wants. I just don't care any more.'

Tom shook his head. He'd had enough of all of this, he really had.

*　　*　　*

Kay and Katrina were having headaches of their own. The comet was threatening to prevent them from seeing the final episode of *Made in Eccles*, which was Katrina's favourite programme of all time. The idea of missing the last episode of the season actually filled her with physical terror. Kay was less worried – she'd come up with the idea of finding a TV in the school and sneaking away when everyone was occupied by staring up at the sky. They could watch the programme in peace and sneak back before anyone even noticed they were gone.

Everyone else, though, was enjoying watching the comet. It started off as a faint glow that grew clearer as it got closer, burning through the night with a flaming tail and a fanfare of tiny flickers of light that peppered the sky.

'Beautiful, aren't they?' said Whitewood. 'The earth must be passing through the comet's tail.'

Behind them, Rhydian and Jana started to giggle. Tom turned to see them both swaying on their feet, wobbling around as if their legs had turned to jelly. Rhydian pitched forward, heading for Segolia's telescope, crashing into it. He would have knocked it to the ground if Miss Parish and the scientist hadn't caught it in time. Rhydian reeled backwards. Tom caught him before he hit the ground.

'You couldn't just leave it, could you?' Shannon said angrily to Rhydian, who was still laughing. 'You don't even care, do you? After everything we've been through! Well, I'm done with this friendship!'

'Easy, Shan,' said Tom, worried. 'There's something weird going on . . .'

Jana was tottering around too, knocking into people as she carried on giggling to herself.

Another meteor shower burst overhead, and at the same time both Rhydian and Jana flopped to the ground, unconscious.

'What happened?' asked Jeffries, coming over. 'Quick – let's get them both inside.'

Whitewood and Tom struggled into the school with Jana while Shannon and Jeffries carried Rhydian, laying both of them on benches in the science lab. Kara followed behind, determined not to be left out.

Shannon looked at Whitewood. This must be a Wolfblood thing, they thought, but what?

'Their vitals and pupil responses are normal,' said Whitewood, covering her panic. 'I think it's just exhaustion. Probably up all night watching TV, you know teenagers!'

At that moment Katrina and Kay appeared, Kay with her arm around her friend. 'She feels faint, sir!' Kay said. 'I think she's got the same thing that they have!'

'Right – bring her in here, then,' said Jeffries, looking more worried by the minute.

'Actually, sir, I feel sick!' said Katrina.

'I'd better get her to the toilets, sir!' said Kay.

'All right,' Jeffries told them, 'just keep me updated, OK?' He pulled his phone out of his pocket. 'Right, I'm calling an ambulance.'

'No!' said Tom and Shannon together.

'They've just fainted, Tim,' Whitewood told him quickly. 'I'll keep them under observation, let you know if there's any change.'

Jeffries nodded. 'OK. I'll check on Katrina. Kara, come on.'

'I'd rather stay here and help, sir,' she said. She had no intention of going anywhere until she knew what was going on. She was tired of being left out of everything just because Shannon thought she was so much smarter than she was.

'Katrina is in the girls' toilets,' Jeffries told her impatiently. 'I need you to come with me.'

As soon as they had gone, Whitewood looked up at Tom and Shannon. 'This is not exhaustion,' she said.

'Yeah, and there's nothing wrong with Katrina,' said Tom. 'You don't think it's because of the comet, do you? Jana said Ceri was freaking out. I'm going to call her . . .'

He got his phone out and dialled, but there was no

answer. 'It might have affected Ceri too – I'll go and check on her.' He went, leaving Shannon and Whitewood to look after Rhydian and Jana.

Sixteen

Dr Whitewood didn't know where to start. She sent Shannon to get some ammonia from the chemical locker to use as smelling salts, just in case Rhydian and Jana had just fainted, but it had no effect at all.

'This is my fault,' Shannon said, getting more upset by the minute. 'I told Rhydian our friendship was over, and look what happened.'

Tom called as soon as he got to the Smiths' place. 'Ceri's out too,' he said. 'She's written something on the floor, though. "Icefire".'

'Icefire?' Shannon repeated.

'That's the comet – the nucleus,' Whitewood said. 'I'm going to call Alex,' she said. 'See if he has any ideas.'

'Stay with Ceri, Tom,' Shannon said, before she hung up.

Kay and Katrina were in heaven. The ploy of feeling sick had worked – they were sitting in front of the final episode of *Made in Eccles*, which was everything they had hoped it would be. Drama, high heels, love triangles

. . . perfect. Or at least, it would be if Kara hadn't found them. She'd gone into the toilets at Jeffries' instruction and covered for the fact that they weren't in there, but then she'd come looking for them – and now she wouldn't shut up.

'Who do these losers think they are?' she asked.

'Shh,' hissed Kay. 'If you're not interested, go back to your comet.'

'I can't, can I? I told Jeffries I was looking after you two idiots.'

'Well, why don't you go and look after Rhydian and Jana, then?' suggested Katrina.

'I would, but I am not part of Team Shannon and Whitewood,' sulked Kara.

Katrina picked up on her tone. 'Oooh – is somebody jealous?'

Kara left, annoyed with her friends. They could be so juvenile sometimes! She went back to the science lab, where, as usual, Shannon and Dr Whitewood stopped talking as soon as she walked into the room.

'What can we do for you?' Whitewood said, as if Kara had no place being there at all.

That was enough to push Kara over the edge. It was obvious they weren't going to tell her what was going on. 'They're still out, then?' she said.

'Clearly,' Whitewood said stonily.

'Right,' said Kara, pulling her phone out of her pocket.

'Who are you calling?' Shannon asked.

Kara stared at her, hard, but didn't say anything until the voice answered on the other end of the line. 'Ambulance, please. Bradlington High.' Then she turned on her heel and walked out, satisfied to see the shocked look on Shannon's face.

'They can't take them to the hospital,' Shannon said to Whitewood, as soon as Kara was gone. 'They'll be in for days. They'll do tests!'

'Then we'd better work out what's wrong before they get here.'

'Right,' said Shannon, looking at Google on her phone. '*Icefire . . . Icefire flies through the sky/Night burns brighter than a star/Bringing darkness from afar.*'

'Sounds like a nursery rhyme,' said Whitewood.

Shannon nodded. 'Like a Wolfblood "Ring-a-Ring-a-Roses". . .'

Whitewood liked the analogy. 'Yes, and the Black Death is our comet – which means it's happened before . . .'

Shannon carried on reading. 'Yes,' she said, 'some scholars think the rhyme's connected to a real event. Two hundred years ago, some villagers in Germany fell into a deep sleep after a great light filled the sky one night.'

'So . . . the villagers were Wolfbloods?' Whitewood surmised.

'And the great light a meteor storm. The thing is . . . the villagers never woke up.'

They both looked at Rhydian and Jana. They couldn't let that happen here. They *had* to find a way to wake them up.

'Comets pass over the earth all the time,' said Shannon.

'But Bayle's Comet would very rarely coincide with a dark moon,' Whitewood pointed out.

'So . . . it's somehow magnifying its effects?'

'But how?'

Shannon was trying to think of an answer when the door opened and Kay and Katrina stumbled in, looking frantic.

'Shannon,' Katrina cried, 'we need your help! The TV signal's gone fuzzy and we've lost *Made in Eccles*!' Kay nudged her hard in the ribs, nodding at Jana and Rhydian. Katrina did actually have the good grace to look embarrassed. 'Which . . . isn't as important as what's going on here, obviously,' she added lamely.

'Yeah,' said Kay, as she and Katrina started to back out of the room. 'It's only a bit of interference . . .'

Shannon and Whitewood stared at each other. 'That's it!' Shannon shouted.

'Interference!' said the scientist, understanding perfectly.

But they were too late. A second later, Mr Jeffries burst into the room, followed by two paramedics. Becca and Shannon moved out of the way as the ambulance team checked over Rhydian and Jana.

'Hypothesis,' Shannon whispered, 'the meteor shower's interfering with whatever links Wolfbloods to the moon . . .'

'And as there's no moon, Wolfbloods are particularly susceptible,' said Whitewood quietly.

'. . . because the link is already at its weakest.'

At the other end of the room, one of the paramedics looked up. 'We're taking them in,' he said. 'We'll just get the stretchers.' They left, along with Jeffries, leaving Shannon and Dr Whitewood in a flat panic.

'We have about a minute,' said Whitewood. 'Any interference would have a particular frequency. What were they watching? If you can find out the channel frequency, I might be able to cancel it out.'

Shannon called Tom as Dr Whitewood rushed to the store cupboard and dragged out a signal generator and a portable aerial. 'Tom,' Shannon said, 'I need you to turn on *Made in Eccles*. I need the frequency . . . See if there's an "information" button, or a "service" menu?'

The paramedics came back in as Whitewood turned on the generator. An undulating sine wave appeared, green on a black background.

'Tom says it's six hundred and fifty,' Shannon told her, as the paramedics began to put Rhydian and Jana on to their stretchers.

Whitewood tried to tune the generator to 650 megahertz. The sine wave reached the correct frequency, but nothing happened. 'We're there!' she muttered to herself. 'Why isn't it working?'

'Wait!' Shannon said, as Rhydian was about to be wheeled from the room. She ran over and bent down to kiss him on the forehead.

A bolt of realisation struck Whitewood and she twisted the generator's dial in the opposite direction. The wave on the screen fluctuated wildly. 'Negative! Minus six hundred and fifty . . .' The signal dipped low enough to reach the frequency.

'I'm sorry,' Shannon was saying tearfully to Rhydian. 'I'm so sorry.'

'For what?' Rhydian asked groggily.

'Everything,' Shannon sobbed. Then she gasped. 'You're awake!'

'Who's awake?' asked Jana, sitting up.

Dr Whitewood took them both to the Smiths' house so that she could look after Ceri too.

'I am really grateful, Doctor Whitewood,' said Rhydian.

The scientist smiled and held out her hand. 'Truce?'

'Truce,' Rhydian agreed, shaking on it.

'Right,' said Whitewood. 'Well, I'd better get back. I'll see you all again sometime – hopefully in different circumstances.'

Jana followed her out to her car. 'Doctor Whitewood. Could you could get me some more information . . . about Segolia?'

She looked at her in surprise. 'You want to work for us?'

'I don't know. Not in science. Something else, maybe?'

'I'm sure there's something Segolia could offer a Wolfblood like you,' Whitewood assured her. 'I'll mention it to Alex.'

Inside, Shannon and Rhydian were talking properly for the first time in days.

'I never set out to hurt you,' Shannon said quietly.

'Look, if you hadn't done your work experience with Whitewood, I'd still be in a coma,' Rhydian pointed out. 'I owe you. You didn't betray me. You just lied to do what you thought was right.'

'You can always trust me,' said Shannon. 'You know that, right?'

Rhydian smiled. 'Come here,' he said, and pulled her into a hug.

Tom was watching from the doorway as Jana came back in. She smiled to see her two friends making up. 'Finally,' she sighed happily.

Tom said nothing, but for some reason he didn't look that pleased.

Seventeen

Segolia was more than happy that Jana had showed an interest in the company. In fact, they were so enthusiastic that they invited the whole group to come in for a day so that they could look around. Rhydian was the only one who turned down the invitation. He was more interested in looking through his dad's file again, even though he'd been through it a hundred times already.

'What I don't understand is that if he did all this, how come I found him scrabbling about in a bin? You'd think if he was that smart he would have had some money. Who *are* you, Dad?' Rhydian muttered. He pointed to the logo on the file – a three-headed wolf. 'You know what Cerberus is? It's a wolf with three heads. Maybe that's him. Three different people in one wolf.'

Jana shook her head. 'I won't go to Segolia if you don't want me to. Or you could come with us?'

'No,' he said, 'you should go. When I know the truth. When I know for sure . . . I'll think about it.'

The car that came to collect Jana, Tom and Shannon was large, black and driven by a man who introduced himself as Alf. Jana felt strange, sitting in the back, being driven about behind tinted windows as if she were one of the celebrities she'd seen pictures of in the magazines the Ks loved to flick through. When they arrived at the Segolia site, Dacia was waiting outside for them with Whitewood and a man that Shannon said was Alex Kincaid.

Jana was stunned at the sheer size of the complex. Dacia smiled, holding out her arm to lead her away from the others. 'Jana – I'll show you around.'

'We still can't get our heads around what you did during the dark moon, can we?' Alex said to Shannon and Becca, as they headed off in a different direction. 'By the way, I'm not one for big pronouncements, but today might just be the most significant day in the history of the Segolia Corporation . . .'

'Er . . .' said Tom, still standing by the car, not sure who to follow as his friends were swept away from him. 'Who should I . . .?'

No one was listening. Dacia was too busy apologising to Jana again for taking samples of Ceri's Wolfblood remedies and Shannon was clearly enthralled by the great Alexander Kincaid. It was as if they'd all forgotten Tom was even there. He might as well have not bothered to come. At that moment, the paved slabs on which he stood erupted. Jets of water shot out of the ground, soaking him. Apparently, he'd chosen to stand on a water feature.

'Oh . . . great!' he muttered, wet through. 'That's just . . . great . . .'

And still, neither of his friends noticed.

Jana had never been anywhere like Segolia in her life. Everything was clean, sterile. It was all so . . . unnatural. Not a hint of greenery anywhere – no plants, no earth.

'I know it's a lot to take in,' Dacia told her, 'but we can help you find your place here.'

'How many of the humans in here know about you?' Jana whispered, as they walked into a busy office.

'None. But we're the most important people Segolia has, and there's never been a wild Wolfblood here before, so believe me, you're a pretty big deal. Oh no,' she said, turning. 'What does she want?'

'So,' said a cold voice behind them. 'This must be the wild Wolfblood I've heard so much about.'

Jana spun around to find a tall, dark woman dressed severely in black, stalking purposefully towards them. Jana had to sniff hard to realise it, but the woman was Wolfblood. Her dark eyes glittered almost as harshly as the light did off her sleek gold jewellery. The room seemed chilled, somehow, as if she carried the cold north wind with her. She was threatening, and Jana didn't need her wolf senses to realise it. She felt her hackles rise.

'Who are you?' she asked.

'This is Victoria Sweeney, our head of security,' said Dacia.

'I think I'm capable of introducing myself,' Sweeney told her. 'The first thing a Wolfblood learns in Segolia is not to act like a Wolfblood. We can't have the humans running for the hills. So don't draw any attention to yourself.' She gave Dacia a hard stare. 'Or I'll hold *you* responsible. Now, come with me.'

'I'm supposed to be giving Jana a tour . . .' Dacia said.

Sweeney glared at Dacia. 'It can wait. This way . . .'

'OK.' Dacia smiled, although Jana thought it seemed forced. Jana wasn't happy at all, but she went along with Sweeney's request.

Alf had taken Tom into the security guards' break room to dry out and warm up, although the corridor seemed to still be under construction – there were cables all over the place.

'What is this place?' Tom asked, narrowly avoiding getting tangled in an electrical cord.

'Head of security's putting in some new servers,' said Alf. 'Keeping even more tabs on us. I'll come back when you're ready and take you to meet the lasses . . .'

'Don't think I'll bother,' Tom said glumly. 'I was wasting my time, anyway. They're only interested in the other two. I'm not a scientist.'

'Right,' said Alf. 'I'll get you when they're finished. There's a TV there. And keep your head down – you're not meant to be up here. I don't want to get dragged up in front of the Sweeney . . . Head of security,' Alf explained, before he left.

Tom flicked on the tiny old portable television. He found a couple of things to watch, but all in all he got pretty bored, just sitting there drying out. He was thinking about settling down for a nap when he heard something outside, in the empty room that was being worked on beyond Alf's hideaway.

'Don't even try it,' he heard a rough voice bark.

Tom got up and looked out of the window to see one of Segolia's security guards roughly pushing a guy across the room. He looked like a delivery man, and as he turned around, Tom could see that his hands were tied behind his back.

Victoria Sweeney had taken Jana and Dacia to a large, empty room and told Jana to sit down at a table that

141

had been placed right in the middle of it. Sweeney handed over a necklace made from a leather thong with a long, slightly yellowed fang threaded on to it.

'All right, wild one,' the security chief said, in a low, threatening voice. 'Let's see you use your "Eolas" – your "Ansion" – and tell me what that is.'

Jana fingered the tooth, but couldn't pick anything up. This place was too unnatural – there was no connection to the wild, no place from whence Eolas could flow to her.

'I can't do it,' she said, eventually. 'It's too hard.'

Sweeney glanced at the security officer who stood next to her, her eyes flashing with triumph. 'Or maybe Eolas and Ansion don't exist? Maybe it's all rubbish?'

'They connect you to nature,' Jana said, losing her patience with this horrible woman. 'They're to use in the wild. Not in a man-made box!'

'Fine,' Sweeney said. 'We can do nature.' She looked up at Dacia and flicked her head as if it were an order.

Dacia disappeared for a few minutes and returned with a tiny knarled and twisted bonsai tree in a pot.

'There,' said Sweeney. 'Natural enough for you?'

Jana ran her fingers through the tiny leaves, shut her eyes and tried to concentrate. She felt the rush of Ansion flooding through her, opening her eyes to images she could only see in her mind. She let the story unfold before she began to speak.

'The tooth is from someone in your pack,' she began. 'Your . . . grandmother. She was pack leader. There was a fire. In a forest . . .'

'Tell me more,' Sweeney said, her voice softer now.

'She was leading the pack away from the flames,' Jana went on. 'But they were moving so quickly. The youngest cub wasn't strong enough to keep up. The alpha decided to leave it behind, so the pack could escape. But the cub survived.' Jana opened her eyes, letting Ansion fade away as she looked at Sweeney. 'She left you this, so you'd always know who you were. But . . . you never found your pack again.'

There was a moment of stunned silence as Sweeney stared at Jana across the table. Then, to Dacia's utter amazement, both the security chief and her guard got down on one knee before Jana.

'There will always be a place for you at Segolia,' said Victoria Sweeney, as her phone rang. She answered it with a harsh, 'Yes?'

Tom was still crouching in Alf's den listening to everything going on outside when Victoria Sweeney turned up.

'What do you know about Cerberus?' she asked the prisoner.

'Never heard of it,' said the man. Then he made a run for it, Sweeney chasing after him and leaving the room empty.

Tom crept out of his hiding place, wondering whether to follow. His foot chinked against something lying on the floor. He bent to pick it up – it was a canister of some kind, or an elaborate syringe. He put it in his pocket.

Eighteen

'Now,' said Kincaid, settling himself into a chair in the laboratory as Shannon and Dr Whitewood looked on. 'You will have probably noticed I'm a bit of a peg-leg. I was born with a degenerative disease for which – really annoyingly – there is no cure.'

Shannon watched as Dr Whitewood got out a small silver instrument case and opened it. Inside was a roughly cylindrical device that looked like a futuristic syringe. Then Becca took a pair of scissors and sliced open the leg of Kincaid's jeans, peeling back the fabric to reveal a nasty-looking scar on the man's leg.

'Which brings me to that cheese and pepperoni number you snaffled away from your friend Jana,' Kincaid went on. 'It could well end up becoming the most significant piece of pizza in history. It was the breakthrough we needed. We used her DNA to synthesise a serum . . .'

Shannon's brain rushed to catch up and make sense of what he was saying. She remembered what Whitewood had said – that Wolfblood DNA could hold the key to curing all kinds of illnesses.

'A serum . . . to repair damaged cells?' she asked.

Kincaid gave a cavalier grin. 'Well, either that or bring on a slow and agonising death . . .' He winked as Whitewood loaded a vial of blue liquid into the syringe.

'Wait,' said Shannon, shocked. 'You're testing it on yourself?

'I can't risk it on anyone else.' He nodded at Dr Whitewood, who activated the device. A bright blue laser beam shot out of the end and straight into Kincaid's leg. 'Cross fingers!' he added cheerfully.

Shannon watched nervously as Whitewood emptied the serum into Kincaid's leg. She half expected something terrible to happen – for him to collapse, or maybe start convulsing. But nothing happened. Nothing bad, anyway.

'How do you feel?' Whitewood asked, a few minutes later.

Kincaid nodded. 'Good,' he said. 'In fact . . .' He got to his feet and started to walk.

He didn't limp. Not even a bit. Not even *slightly*.

'I can't believe it,' whispered Whitewood.

'Has it – has it worked already?' Shannon asked, astounded.

Kincaid laughed, walking around the lab. 'I thought there might be a little improvement. But nothing like this . . .'

Whitewood could hardly contain herself. 'This is just

the start,' she said excitedy. 'Think what we might be able to do! Cure blindness, deafness. Help paralysed people to walk again . . .'

'And all because of a cheese and pepperoni pizza,' said Kincaid, before turning to look at Shannon. 'And you.'

Shannon was the happiest she had ever been in her life.

Later, once the day was over, they all convened at the Kafe so that they could tell Rhydian about their day. That was when Tom produced the gizmo he'd found.

'I've got no idea what it is,' he said, as they all stared at it. 'But here's the best part. "The Sweeney" asked the fella if he knew anything about,' here Tom paused for maximum effect, '. . . "Cerberus".'

Rhydian almost leapt right across the table, just as Tom had known he would. 'That's what they're after my dad for! So . . . he wasn't working alone?'

'Or,' said Tom, 'there's something else going on. The Sweeney didn't want anyone to know about this prisoner, right? Why would she do that if she had nothing to hide?'

'Whatever you saw Victoria do might not be as bad as you think,' warned Jana.

Tom looked at her as if she'd lost her marbles. 'A bloke being tied up?'

'This is similar to the one Becca used on Alex,' Shannon said, looking at the device. 'We need to tell them.'

'And what if they're involved, too?' Rhydian asked.

Shannon shook her head with complete certainty. 'There's no way.'

'Oh, really?' asked Tom, pointing at the device. 'Then how do you explain this thing? You just said it's the same. We can't trust anyone over there. And even if we do trust them, the Sweeney might go after them.'

Jana stepped in. 'Look,' she said. 'Victoria's the head of security. She protects Wolfbloods. How do you know this guy wasn't a threat? To all of us?'

'Or maybe you can't see what's staring you in the face,' Rhydian suggested, his patience running out.

Jana bristled at his tone. 'What's that supposed to mean?'

'It means, that maybe Segolia's not the great place you're both making it out to be and my dad was telling the truth.'

Shannon snorted. 'Well, maybe your dad's not so innocent in all of this. You're making up theories to suit your own agenda.'

'I'm just looking at the facts,' said Rhydian.

'What facts?' Shannon asked, her temper rising too. 'I trust Alex and Becca, and you're just looking for ways to get back at me over that.'

Rhydian stood up and pushed his way out of the booth. 'It's not about you, Shannon! It's about my dad!' He walked out of the Kafe.

Shannon turned on Tom, frustrated. 'This is your fault. Why'd you have to stir things up?'

Tom stood up and pocketed the device, walking out without another word. He'd had enough of all of them, Shannon in particular. She was supposed to be his best friend, but she'd conveniently forgotten that if she hadn't gone off without him that morning, he'd never have ended up with this thing in the first place! Her and her precious Segolia – she was welcome to them.

Tom went home and mooched about in his bedroom for a bit. Then he took the device out and examined it. His finger caught against a button and accidentally pressed it. The thing whirred into life, lights flashing, just for a moment . . . then died again. Tom sighed. It had probably been broken when it was dropped earlier. He turned it over, listening for a rattle . . .

There was a sudden flash and the device sent a bright blue pulse straight into his chest.

Nineteen

Rhydian had calmed down by the next morning. So had Shannon and Jana.

'We're sorry,' said Jana, as she and Shannon came to a stop beside the bench where he sat in the school grounds, watching Jimi, Sam, Liam and a bunch of others play an early morning game of football.

'Yeah,' said Shannon.

'I still don't think you're right about Victoria,' said Jana, 'but I don't want us to fall out over it.'

Rhydian got up to hug them both. 'That's why we're a pack,' he said.

Tom shattered their reunion. He rode his bike right into the middle of the football pitch and leapt off. In one smooth movement he intercepted the ball, danced around Jimi and Liam and booted it straight past the keeper.

'Get in!' he whooped, triumphant, before launching into an astonishing series of back flips.

The others looked on with their mouths open as Tom finally came to a stop.

'How did you do that?' asked Liam, as they all gathered,

cheering and jostling. Tom shrugged with a grin, totally pumped and full of energy.

'OK, superstar,' said Jimi, 'I'll give you twenty quid if you can kick this through Jeffries' window.'

Tom glanced up to Jeffries' office. It looked like an impossible shot, but a second later Tom had grabbed the ball, hopped backwards and launched into a kick. The ball soared into a high, graceful curve, shooting straight through Jeffries' window. There was a faint crash from inside.

Everyone ran before Jeffries had a chance to look out.

Shannon grabbed Tom outside their form room, pulling him over to Rhydian and Jana. 'What's going on?'

'Nothing,' Tom said. He was sniffing the air. 'Ew – BO. Can you smell that?'

Jana looked at Rhydian, who frowned and asked, 'What else can you smell?'

Tom sniffed again. 'Well . . . seven different perfumes. Some sweaty socks. Karrina's just bleached her roots – I thought she was a natural blonde!' He paused, and then added, 'SBD – fifteen minutes ago, aaaaand . . . savoury mince for lunch.'

Shannon was staring at him with a look of utter horror. 'You took the serum, didn't you?'

Tom shrugged, still buzzing, talking far faster than usual. 'It was an accident. I was messing about and it just went off . . .' He loomed into Rhydian's face. 'Why do you do this, "It's so hard being a Wolfblood" thing when it feels so *good*?'

'Tom,' said Shannon, on the verge of panic. 'We have no idea what was in that serum. You need to get yourself to a hospital!'

'Back off,' Tom warned her. 'I haven't done anything wrong, yeah?'

He went into the form room, enjoying the cheer that went up – people were talking about his football feat. It was the first time in – well, ever, really – that Tom had been the centre of attention. He loved it. What was the problem? He felt fantastic!

His friends watched as Tom became someone they didn't recognise. At lunchtime he even squared up to Sam, pinning him against the wall and forcing him to give Kay's phone back to her after he'd nicked it. The three Ks were amazed at this 'new' Tom – 'so cool' they called him – not to his face, obviously, but since he could hear everything, he heard it anyway.

Not knowing what else to do, Rhydian called Dacia. She arrived just as Bradlington High was turning out for the day, but she didn't know what to do either.

'I can't get a Wolfblood doctor here without Sweeney finding out,' she said. 'I don't know how to help, not in secret. I'm sorry.'

Rhydian decided that if she was going to be useless with Tom, she could at least help him with something else.

'What do you know about Cerberus, Dacia?' he asked.

She blinked, surprised by the change of subject. 'I . . . gave you the file,' she said.

'And that's it? That's all you know? Who gave you the file?'

Dacia swallowed nervously. 'Sweeney,' she admitted.

'Don't you get it?' Rhydian asked, exasperated. 'Dad obviously found the connection between her and Cerberus – whatever it is – so she goes after him and sets him up. *That's* why she gave you that file. To stop me asking questions like this.'

Beside him, Jana shifted uncomfortably from one foot to another. Rhydian could be right.

'I had no reason not to believe her,' Dacia protested. 'Even if you're right, I can't just come out and accuse her. I wouldn't last five minutes!'

'Then be a Wolfblood,' Rhydian suggested, with a hint of disgust. 'Use a bit of cunning. You're on the inside. We're not. Or do you like being manipulated?'

Dacia gave up. 'All right!' she said, walking away. 'I'll see what I can find out.'

Shannon watched as Tom headed for the school gates, surrounded by his peers and with his arm draped around

Kay's shoulders. She'd changed her tune. It looked as if they were getting back together after all. 'So what do we do about Tom?' she asked.

At that moment Tom saw Dacia getting into her car and let go of Kay, coming over with a frown.

'What's Dacia doing here?' he asked.

'We're worried about you,' said Shannon, pulling out her phone. 'You need professional help. I'm calling Alex and Becca.'

Tom grabbed her arm, hard, surprising her. 'Don't stick your nose in my business! There's nothing wrong with me.'

'You don't know that,' Shannon said, as Kay, Katrina and Kara appeared.

'What *is* your problem?' Kay said, to Shannon. 'No one likes a green-eyed monster.'

'No problem,' Shannon said, her own temper rising. If hanging out with Kay was what Tom wanted, who was she to care? 'Not any more. He's on his own.'

'No,' Kay said, slipping her arm into Tom's, 'he's with *me*, Shannon.'

Shannon walked off, Rhydian and Jana trailing behind.

'You all right?' Kay asked Tom.

'Yeah,' he said. 'Just . . . give me a minute . . .'

He ran after his three former friends, finding them in one of the school's empty corridors.

'Hey!' he called after them. 'Do you want to know something?'

Tom waited until all three of them had turned around. He wanted their full, undivided attention for a change.

'I'm glad that I took it,' he said. 'I'm sick and tired of playing second fiddle to *your* Wolfblood dramas,' he said, pointing at Rhydian, 'to *your* desperation to prove yourself,' he said to Shannon, 'and to *your* inability to cope with modern life,' he said to Jana.

'Tom,' said Rhydian, taking a step forward.

'Don't "Tom" me, OK!' Tom shouted. 'Tom's always the one picking up the pieces, lying for you lot, being a shoulder to cry on – and if I'm not doing that, I might as well be invisible. Well, not any more.'

With that, he left them standing there and headed back out to join Kay.

Twenty

The Tom situation just got more and more worrying. He wouldn't listen to anyone, least of all Shannon, Rhydian and Jana. The next day they arrived at school to find the whole class gathered in the playground, cheering as they watched Tom turn a series of ever-more-dangerous somersaults on the roof of the sports centre.

'Just when you thought things couldn't get any worse,' said Shannon, terrified that he'd fall and break his neck.

'Get down! Right now!' shouted Jeffries' voice over the crowd as he strode across the playground. The teacher had to dole out four detentions in a row before Tom finally climbed to the ground amid another storm of adoring applause.

'Total ledge!' said Liam, clapping him on the back.

'What is this?' Jeffries stormed. 'The cult of Tom Okanawe?'

'I will be right there in detention with you, mate,' said Jimi, reaching out to shake Tom's hand. 'It's not a punishment, it's an honour!'

'You're lucky you didn't kill yourself, you idiot!' said

Shannon, her anxious voice splashing over them all like a bucket of ice-cold water. Tom scowled at her.

Jimi shook his head. 'You know what your problem's always been, don't you, Tom?' he said, pointing at Shannon. 'Sour-face over there.'

Shannon looked at Tom as everyone around her sniggered, expecting him to defend her the way he always did against Jimi's jibes. But he didn't say a thing, and that hurt her more than anything Jimi Chen could say.

'Office!' yelled Jeffries, leading the way as Tom's fans cheered him on once again. Tom bunched his hands into fists and raised them in triumph as he followed Jeffries across the playground.

He left Jeffries' office after the teacher had finished a rant that Tom had absolutely no interest in listening to, and ran straight into the Ks.

'I'm going to be at the Kafe later tonight,' said Kay, fiddling with her hair as she looked at him. 'If you're going to be around?'

Tom hid a grin. What was the saying? Treat 'em mean, keep 'em keen, right? 'Yeah,' he said coolly. 'I'll be there . . . Katrina already asked me, so . . .'

With that he swaggered off, listening to the explosion as Katrina tried to defend herself to her friend. *So this is what it is like to have girls fight over you,* he thought. *It's great!*

Rhydian, Jana and Shannon had watched the whole exchange. Jana shook her head. 'We should have called Whitewood straight away,' she said. 'She'd know what was in that serum.'

Shannon started walking, trying not to care. 'Tom doesn't want our help,' she said. 'He's made that perfectly clear.'

Rhydian caught her by the arm and pulled her to a stop. 'That's not the real Tom. The real Tom's somewhere underneath. I don't think this is going to go away by itself,' he added, seeing Shannon's face soften. 'Call Whitewood. Tell her to get here as quickly as she can.'

He went after Tom to try to talk some sense into him. He found his friend in the boys' toilets, staring at himself in the mirror.

'I get it,' Rhydian told him. 'Strong is good. But what you're not getting is it's knowing what to do with it.'

Tom turned to face him, shaking his head. 'You hate this, don't you? Cos you always have to be the special one.'

'Mate, that is ridiculous.'

'*Mate,*' said Tom in a low, dangerous voice as he stepped so close to Rhydian that he was right in his face. 'I'm not like you. I'm *better* than you. I can do anything

158

you can – full moon, dark moon. Anytime. I'm *more* than a Wolfblood.'

Tom pushed past Rhydian and went out into the corridor, where Jana and Shannon were waiting. 'You're not taking this off me,' he told them. 'It's *mine*.'

Rhydian came out and watched Tom strut away. 'Whitewood?' he asked Shannon.

'It went straight to voicemail.'

Rhydian made a decision. 'I'm going down there.'

'What? To Segolia?'

'Sweeney's behind all this,' Rhydian told Shannon. 'She'll know what's in that serum.'

'So what?' Jana asked. 'You're just going to walk in there and ask her what's going on? I used Ansion. I know her history, her ancestry. I don't think she's the bad wolf.'

'It's like the Segolia fan club round here!' Rhydian exclaimed. 'She's going to tell me what is in Tom's veins. She's going to tell me why she framed my dad. And I'm not leaving until she does.' He walked off, determined.

'I'll keep an eye on him,' Jana said to Shannon. 'You look after Tom.'

Shannon nodded. 'OK. See you later!'

Tom sat in French class with Shannon on one side of him and the three Ks on the other. Even with his headphones on he could hear Katrina and Kay arguing about

159

him. Meanwhile, Shannon was busily repeating French sentences and glancing at him every few minutes as if he'd grown another head. He tried to ignore her and follow the instructions the voice on the programme was giving him. But after a few minutes the voice seemed to be getting louder. He tried to turn it down, but he couldn't – and then it seemed to speed up, speaking louder, faster and faster, overlapping and echoing and –

He dragged off the headphones and stood up, dizzy and disorientated, breathing hard. 'Miss!' he gasped, 'I'm going to be sick!'

The class all laughed, assuming this was another one of the new Tom's stunts, but Shannon stood up and added. 'It's his allergies, miss! I told him there were nuts in nut loaf! I'll take him to the nurse . . .'

Shannon hooked one of Tom's arms over her shoulder and hugged him around the waist, trying to keep him upright as they stumbled down the corridor and out into the playground. Outside, she leaned him against the iron girder that supported the walkway out of the main building.

'I'm OK . . .' Tom mumbled.

'You're not OK! You're about as far from OK as you are from Australia!'

Tom gave a cheeky grin and leaned forward as if he might fall over. 'I could run to Australia, you know.'

160

'Tom,' Shannon said, pushing him back and putting her hands to his face to hold him there. 'Just *breathe*.'

Tom finally did as he was told, his breathing beginning to even out as he calmed down. He almost looked as if he were waking up as he realised where they were and how close Shannon was standing.

'Argh!' he shouted, pushing her away. 'Get off me.'

'Right,' said Shannon, making a decision, 'I'm taking you home, so I can keep an eye on you. I'll figure out what to tell the school later. You need to keep out of sight till this passes. If this passes . . .'

Tom's phone beeped and he took it out. It was a message from Kay, asking if he was coming to the Kafe later.

'Tom, will you just ignore that?' Shannon asked.

'It's from Kay . . .' Tom said, sending a quick reply that said: SURE AM!'

'Tom,' Shannon said again, trying to get his attention. 'There must be a tiny part of your brain left that can understand the concept of side-effects!'

Tom was distracted by his phone again – another message from Kay.

Shannon shook her head. 'Is that as good as it gets? Kay texting you?'

Tom gave her a look. 'I like her. And *you* are not messing this up for me again. Nothing is messing this up for me.'

Shannon threw up her hands, exasperated. 'You've got bigger problems than getting back with Kay!'

Tom lost his temper. 'Well, that'd make a change, wouldn't it, Shannon? All I have ever had is average problems. Average looks, average grades, average everything. Actually, you know what? Average would be an improvement!' he said angrily, to Shannon's stunned face. 'Below average, that's me. Below-average boy looking forward to a below-average future . . .' He looked her in the eye and added, 'With below-average *friends*.'

With that he pushed past her and went back into school, leaving Shannon blinking back tears.

Rhydian and Jana's trip to Segolia didn't go too well, either. Dacia met them in reception, extremely nervous, and told them she had no information – either that could help Tom, or about Rhydian's dad.

'It's only been one day!' she protested.

'Fine,' said Rhydian loudly, determined not to be put off. 'Then get Sweeney down here.'

'You want me to be the next one she carts off?' asked Dacia. 'Because then you'll never know the truth about your dad, will you? All you're doing is making this harder for me to do it unnoticed.'

Rhydian tried to calm down. 'Tom's really messed up,' he said. 'I don't know what else to do.'

'I can't help that your friend walked out of here with that serum. Or that he was stupid enough to try it,' Dacia pointed out. 'You asked me to find out if your dad was right. That's what I'm trying to do.'

'And if Tom gets sick? Or worse?'

'I thought he was going to Whitewood?'

'We can't get hold of her,' said Jana.

'Then you'd better keep trying,' said Dacia. 'The longer you keep me here the less I can do to help. You need to leave now before you put us all in jeopardy.'

Rhydian and Jana left. They were crossing Segolia's rain-wet flagstones, discussing what to do next, when a car screeched to a halt in front of them.

'Get in!' yelled Rebecca Whitewood.

When school let out, Shannon went straight to the Smiths' place. Rhydian, Jana and Whitewood were already waiting there with Ceri.

'You told me on a *voicemail* what your friend had stolen from Segolia,' said Rebecca, clearly agitated. 'There are cameras everywhere. I've just been telling these two how stupid they've been!'

Shannon's only worry was Tom. 'Look, he had a real freak out in French class,' she said. 'It was like an attack.'

'Right,' said Whitewood. 'You'd better take me to him straight away.'

'He's at the Kafe. With Kay.'

Shannon watched as all of them except Ceri rushed out to Whitewood's car.

'You're not going with them?' Ceri asked.

Shannon tried to smile. 'He doesn't want me around. Or I don't want to be around him.' She shrugged. 'One or the other.'

'Because of this . . . Kay?' Ceri asked. 'You – do not like her stepping on your territory?'

Shannon frowned, completely taken aback. 'Tom's not my territory!'

'Oh,' Ceri said, going to the sink. 'Right.'

Shannon stared at the table in front of her. Despite what Tom had said, did she really want to leave him to deal with all of this without her? Did she want to just . . . leave him to Kay, who didn't even know the real Tom the way she did?

She got up and ran after the others.

Twenty-one

At the Kafe, the night was just getting started, although Tom was having trouble concentrating on what Kay was saying. Everything was a distraction – every conversation from every corner of the room, every smell . . . they all bombarded him at once, vying for his attention until there was too much in his head for Tom to be able to tell one thing from another.

'All right, mate?' said a familiar voice behind him. 'Date night's over.'

Tom glanced over his shoulder to see Rhydian, Jana and Shannon.

'We've brought help,' Shannon told him quietly, and that was when Tom saw Whitewood, lurking by the door.

'Look,' Tom said, 'I don't need your kind of help.'

'Don't make a scene,' Rhydian warned. 'You're coming with us.'

Tom stood up and pushed away from the bar, going to the jukebox instead. 'I can do anything I want,' he said, as he punched in a number and a song began to play. 'Turn it up!' he yelled to Katrina, getting into the groove.

The café came to a standstill as Tom began to dance. He danced up to a stunned Kay, pulling her from her stool and spinning her around the room. From the corner of his eye he could see people filming him as others clapped and cheered. Tom jumped on to a table and lifted Kay up to dance with him, feeling completely invincible. Who cared if his old friends were staring at him as if he'd gone completely mad? This was the new Tom, and he was awesome . . .

With a renewed burst of energy, Tom lifted Kay again, intending to spin her around, but he lost his grip. She screamed as she flew across the room, crashing into Katrina and Kara and sending all three girls into a heap on the sofa, which then tipped backwards and crashed to the floor.

Tom suddenly felt dizzy. His eyesight blurred and he struggled down from the table, trying to focus. He felt suddenly confused. This was the Kafe, wasn't it? Why was everyone looking at him? Something fizzed in his bloodstream – something looming inside him, growing, *growling* . . .

Tom fled for the door, only to crash into Mr Jeffries, who was just coming in.

'Whoa!' said the teacher, trying to stop him as the

others appeared behind. Jeffries was even more confused when he saw Whitewood. 'Rebecca?'

Tom lashed out. 'Get off me! Let me go!'

Jeffries caught hold of Tom's wrists as he flailed – just as the yellow surge of the wolf lit up Tom's eyes. Jeffries stopped dead in shock, blinking, and his hesitation was enough to let Tom slip out of his grasp. He ran across the square, heading for the woods.

'I'll – I'll call you!' Whitewood called to Jeffries, as she ran after Rhydian, Jana and Shannon, who were all shouting for Tom to stop.

Tom didn't stop, not until he was deep into the forest. Then he collapsed in a heap, unconscious and unresponsive.

'He's burning up,' said Whitewood, checking him over. 'His heart's racing . . .'

Shannon was pale. 'Is he OK?'

Whitewood didn't answer. She searched Tom's jacket and pulled out the device he'd taken from Segolia, frowning at it. 'It's definitely one of ours. I've no way of telling what was in it. Our serum can't be doing this to him . . .'

'If you didn't make it, who did?' Rhydian asked.

'*Is he OK?*' Shannon asked again, not caring about anything but Tom.

Whitewood shook her head. 'Not if these symptoms continue.' She took out her phone and hit a number on speed dial. There was no choice – if this kid was to survive, she needed help and Alex Kincaid was the only person she could call.

They took Tom back to the Smiths' house and laid him on blankets in the living room. He was out cold, his breathing was fast and shallow and his temperature far, far too high. When Kincaid arrived he immediately wanted to see the device that had injected Tom.

'I don't get this,' Kincaid frowned, as he looked at the syringe. 'I don't get how anyone could get hold of our equipment.'

Whitewood nodded at the others. 'They think Victoria Sweeney is involved. But I don't get how even she could . . .'

Kincaid looked up, as if realising something. 'The missing batch, remember? Who looked into that? Who came down to the lab and said to leave it to her?'

Whitewood stared at him. 'The same person who monitors every transaction, everyone and everything . . .'

It was Jana who said what they were all thinking. 'Victoria Sweeney.' It seemed that Rhydian's suspicions had been completely correct all along.

Kincaid pulled out another syringe loaded with a different serum and went to inject Tom with it.

'It's just something I've been working on,' he said, as he shot it into Tom's chest.

168

They all watched, tensely. At first nothing happened – Tom's breathing stayed harsh and fast. But then he seemed to relax. His breathing started to slow, returning to normal. His eyelids started to flutter, as if he were beginning to come round.

Shannon let out a sigh of relief.

But then Tom began to convulse. His eyes opened, burning yellow, and he opened his mouth and arched his back, howling. The others held him down.

'It must have reacted with the serum he took earlier!' shouted Kincaid.

Shannon stood back, helpless and scared. Then a thought occurred to her. 'Wolfblood healing!' she said to Ceri. 'He's got Wolfblood DNA in him – maybe Wolfblood remedies will work!'

Kincaid ignored her. 'I'll take him to Segolia. There will be questions, but I'll take responsibility.'

'No! We're running out of time!' Shannon cried, desperate. 'Ceri – *please!*'

Ceri nodded. 'Get my things,' she said to Jana, before kneeling beside Tom, whose eyes fluttered open, pained and pulsing a sick yellow.

'Help me,' he whispered.

'Just breathe,' Ceri told him, as Jana reappeared with her medicine bag. She pulled out a pot full of white paste and began to chant as she painted it over his forehead and cheeks. '*Duwies iacha fe, duwies iacha fe, duwies iacha fe, duwies iacha fe . . .*'

Tom's eyes drifted shut and he began to calm. The black lines tracing his veins began to recede. Eventually Ceri sat back.

'Now we wait,' she said.

Ceri sent everyone out, but she let Shannon stay. Shannon couldn't bear the idea of Tom lying here on the floor on his own, teetering between life and death. Tom couldn't die. He mustn't . . .

'I am going to be so annoyed with you if you leave me,' she told him. 'And don't think it gets you out of saying sorry, because it doesn't.'

She knelt beside him on the floor, tears sliding down her face as she touched her fingers to his cheeks. This time he couldn't push her away. Shannon almost wished he would. At least then she'd know he was alive.

'Who were you trying to impress, Tom?' she asked. 'A bunch of people you don't even like? Fancy, *yes*. Like, I don't think so. It's not the same thing . . .' She stroked his forehead. 'You know where you're going wrong?' she added. 'This whole "below average" thing. You might think you're below average, but I don't. I don't compare you to anyone else, see? You're just you. You're not below anything. You *are* an idiot. But you're *my* idiot.

170

And you're not . . .' Her voice almost gave out. She lay down next to him on the blanket, keeping one arm around him. 'You're not below,' she whispered, into his ear.

'Um,' said Tom awkwardly, a moment later. 'So . . . I'm kind of awake here. Didn't really know when to butt in . . .'

Shannon leapt up, so delighted to tell the others that she didn't even have time to feel embarrassed.

As the others checked Tom over, Rhydian went to talk to Kincaid. 'You really don't know what was in it?' he asked, as the scientist packed away the device that Tom had used.

'I'll take it back with me,' Kincaid assured him. 'Get the residue analysed. We'll find out.'

'Aren't you taking a big risk?'

Kincaid gave a lopsided smile. 'Bit late to worry now. Anyway – I'm not afraid of Victoria Sweeney. You leave her to me.'

Rhydian watched him for another moment. There was something really likeable about Alex Kincaid, and he'd done his best to help with Tom, which was more than he could say of his fellow Wolfblood, Dacia, wasn't it?

'Have you ever heard of . . . Cerberus?' Rhydian asked.

Kincaid looked up at him, puzzled. 'Heard of *what*?'

171

Rhydian took a deep breath. Then he told Kincaid the whole story.

Much later, once Whitewood and Kincaid had gone and Tom had fallen asleep, Shannon, Rhydian and Jana sat together on the sofa in the house, watching TV. They were all tired, but none of them wanted to go home. What had happened to Tom had shaken them all, and no one more than Shannon. She'd known Tom almost her entire life, and the idea of him suddenly not being there any more had opened something up in her that she hadn't realised was there until it was almost too late.

Tom appeared in the doorway, wrapped in a blanket. They watched him for a moment, a little nervous. Was he really back to normal? He moved into the room slowly, his face glowering in the darkness.

'I,' he said, in a very low, slow voice. 'Am more Wolfblood than anyone else here . . .'

Shannon's heart nearly stopped. It hadn't worked after all . . .

Tom's face broke into a smile. 'Jokes! Jokes!' he laughed. 'You lot . . .'

'Moron,' Shannon said, trying to calm herself down.

'Idiot,' agreed Rhydian.

'Not funny,' Jana told him, as Tom squashed himself on to the couch between Shannon and Rhydian.

They all looked at him expectantly. 'What?' Tom asked.

'Oh, I don't know – maybe a thank you would be nice?' Rhydian suggested.

'Well,' said Tom, 'if you lot hadn't left me on my own at Segolia in the first place . . .' He held up his hands as they all pelted him with cushions. 'OK, OK! Thank you! Sorry!'

Rhydian stood up. 'Well, I'm going to get something to eat,' he said.

Jana followed him out, making rude gestures at Tom as she went, leaving him and Shannon alone.

They sat in silence for a minute or two. Tom had been thinking about what Shannon had said when she'd thought he was unconscious, and he knew he had to say something – he just wasn't sure what.

'So, er – about what you said,' he began. 'I mean, I . . . I mean, I do – I just think . . .' He sighed and tried again. 'The truth is, you were right. I mean, that wasn't me, was it? It was actually pretty horrible. So – I'm sorry. And thank you – and I'm not just saying it because they told me to either, OK?'

They stared into each others' eyes – and Shannon realised that yes, this really was the old Tom back again. *Her* Tom. Except that this time, they seemed to be looking at each other just a little differently than they ever had before, and suddenly her heart was –

173

'Get some sleep,' she said quietly, because to say anything else right then would have been too confusing. 'Wake up tomorrow. All this . . . will seem like a distant memory.'

Tom blinked. 'Yeah,' he said. He watched her go out into the kitchen. 'Yeah.'

Twenty-two

Tom sat in Jeffries' office, hoping against hope that their plan to explain his crazy behaviour was going to come off. The teacher was holding the letter from his mum in one hand, shaking his head slightly as he read it.

'Hypoglycaemia?' Jeffries asked, incredulous.

'Yes, sir,' said Tom. 'Apparently, the symptoms include reckless and aggressive behaviour . . . I'm not proud of what happened, sir. But I wasn't in control. It was all pretty scary.'

Jeffries sighed. 'Look, Tom, under any other circumstances, you'd be suspended, if not expelled. But given the medical explanation, and the fact we're so close to exam time . . . I'm going to give you one last chance. One.'

'Yes!' Shannon said, relieved, hugging Tom as soon as he left the office. She'd been waiting outside with Jana and Rhydian. Together, they all headed out into the playground.

'I'd like to thank my resident artist and handwriting

175

forger,' Tom said, speech-like, to Rhydian, 'my scientific advisor,' he went on, nodding at Shannon, who curtseyed with a grin, 'and my mum's hospital stationery. Thank you, Mumsy!'

'You'd better hope he doesn't mention this to her,' Shannon warned him. 'If they find out you intercepted an official school letter and faked a reply, you will be in *so* much trouble . . .'

A loud humming sound floated across the playground. They all turned to see where it was coming from and saw the three Ks, dressed in yoga gear, sitting on mats in the corner, omming loudly to themselves. A small crowd had gathered and Tom, Shannon, Jana and Rhydian went to join it.

'Oh,' said Jimi, pushing through the crowd to see what was going on. 'I thought someone was torturing a cat. Or a boy band . . .'

Everyone laughed. Katrina opened her eyes. 'Laugh all you want,' she said smugly. 'We've taken up yoga to calm our minds before the exams.'

'Meditation helps you stay calm and serene,' Kara added. 'And helps you focus.'

The girls started chanting again, only for Jimi to join in, exaggerating the sounds into a discordant howl, holding his guts as if he had bellyache.

'Leave them alone, Jimi,' Tom said.

Kay's eyes flicked open, staring at him angrily. 'We don't need your help, mad boy.'

'Ignore them, Tom,' Shannon told him. 'As soon as another episode of *Made in Eccles* comes out they'll forget all about you.'

But Tom didn't want Kay to forget about him. He tried to get her attention as they went into the form room. Jeffries had a speech to make about the exams, but all Tom wanted to do was apologise. His attempts to talk to her backfired, though.

'What you do during this period could radically affect your grades,' Jeffries was saying. 'So stay focused, work hard and keep calm . . .'

'Sir,' Kay said, as Tom tried to speak to her yet again, '*you* try keeping calm with a mad boy like Tom pestering you!'

The whole class burst out laughing.

'That's enough,' Jeffries said, and then he said to the Ks, 'You three – stay behind to talk to me, would you?'

The remainder of the class filed out. Rhydian was one of the last to leave the room, which is why he heard what Jeffries said.

'It's Tom I wanted to talk to you about, actually.'

Rhydian's ears pricked up. Why was Jeffries asking the Ks about Tom? He slid to a halt and the others looked around to see what he was doing. Jana joined him by the door, listening too, as Shannon and Tom waited.

'I know Tom hasn't been his usual self lately,' the teacher was saying. 'But what I'm interested in is anything, well . . . more than just "not right". It's anything *really* unusual.'

Rhydian and Jana looked at each other, alarmed. This was not good at all.

'I mean,' the teacher went on, 'anything . . . well, a medical symptom. For example, I don't know, Tom's eyes glowing or changing colour?'

Rhydian looked up at Tom in shock. Jeffries must have seen Tom's eyes wolfing out!

The Ks obviously didn't have anything useful to say, but things got even worse during geography. Mr Jeffries knocked on the door and asked to speak to Liam. Rhydian and Jana strained to hear what was being said outside in the corridor.

'Am I in trouble, sir?' Liam asked.

'No, Liam, I just want to ask you a few questions. About Tom.'

'What are you asking me for, sir?' asked Liam, confused. 'Why don't you ask Rhydian or Jana or Shannon? They're his mates.'

'That's the reason I'm asking someone outside his group of friends,' said Jeffries. 'If someone's in trouble, friends close ranks to protect each other. But sometimes that's the worst thing to do. I want to help Tom – but I need to get to the truth.'

'Truth about what, sir?' Liam asked, still confused.

Jeffries paused for a moment. Rhydian didn't like where this was going at all. 'That's where I think you can help me . . .' He took a deep breath. 'Let's talk about what happened a while back. When you thought Maddy Smith was a werewolf.'

'Sir,' Liam asked, in disbelief, 'are you saying that you think Tom . . . might be a *werewolf*?'

Rhydian and Jana held their breath as they waited for Jeffries to answer. It seemed to take forever until he spoke again.

'Sir?' Liam prompted. 'Are you?'

'No,' Jeffries said eventually. 'No, of course not. Get back to class.'

Liam cast Tom a strange look as he walked past him to get to his desk.

'What is going on?' Tom asked, completely in the dark.

Rhydian turned around with a serious look. 'Jeffries thinks you're a werewolf,' he hissed.

The first chance they all had, they ducked into the darkroom to work out what to do. They had to come up with an excuse for Tom's yellow eyes that wouldn't contradict the fake letter they'd sent to Jeffries from Tom's mum.

'What can possibly explain yellow eyes?' Rhydian asked helplessly.

They all thought. Shannon was pacing around the room. 'Contact lenses!' she exclaimed. 'Like the ones you get in joke shops – for Hallowe'en!' She pointed at Tom. 'You wore yellow contact lenses to give the Ks a fright – for a joke – but they scratched your eye – and that made you aggressive, because of the hypoglycemia – which is what we said in the letter!'

'But . . . How do we know he'll believe that?' Tom asked.

Shannon grinned. 'He will if he sees you with the contact lenses in.'

Rhydian nodded, smiling too. 'I bet the Bradlington Party Shop sells them. I'll get them after school.'

'You can do it tomorrow, in class,' Jana said. 'Make it look like you're playing a trick on us. Sorted!'

Everyone was relieved, especially Tom. He couldn't believe he'd almost screwed everything up again. He got up to leave.

'Where are you going?' Rhydian asked.

'To speak to Kay.'

'Can't that wait?' Shannon asked, disappointed that he was going to run off when they'd just narrowly escaped disaster.

'Get off my back, OK?' Tom snapped at her. 'It's not easy hiding the truth from someone you want to be honest with.' He threw a glance at Rhydian, who couldn't help but nod. He knew what that was like.

But Kay didn't want to listen to a word Tom said. Or rather, what she wanted him to tell her wasn't something he had any right to say.

'It's not just what happened in the Kafe, is it, Tom?' she said, when he interrupted one of the Ks' yoga sessions. 'First we're going out. Then you dump me for Jana. Then you ask me to forgive you – which I do. Then you turn all bad boy and we're like a couple again. Then you go all Terminator on me. And now you're all soft again, like the old Tom. So go on, explain that. Explain how it all makes sense, because you're doing my head in!'

Being honest with her would have meant giving away a secret that wasn't his to give. What was Tom supposed to do? So he just walked out before he could say something he'd regret.

The plan was for Rhydian to go to the party shop after school, pick up the lenses and then meet the others back at the Smiths' place, where Tom and Shannon would be helping Jana with her exam revision. But halfway home, Jana realised something.

'Jeffries is following us,' she whispered.

181

'What?' Tom looked around to see the teacher dragging his bike behind a tree to hide.

'Don't!' Shannon whispered. 'Just act normally, keep him on our tail. When Rhydian gets back, we'll put on a show for him. This is perfect . . .'

They carried on walking, chatting about what Jana would need for the exams. But as they got to the driveway of the house, Jana stopped dead, sniffing hard. Shannon looked around for Jeffries, but there was no sign of him. Jana dumped her bag on the ground and dashed for the front door.

Shannon and Tom rushed after her, into the kitchen. Ceri was sitting at the table with Victoria Sweeney standing calmly in front of her. Two security guards were at Ceri's back. She was clearly a prisoner.

'What are you doing here?' Jana snarled, her blood veining with the wolf as her eyes yellowed. 'Let her go!'

Sweeney took no notice, turning calmly to look at Tom instead. 'The serum you took. Where is it?'

Tom swallowed. 'Gone. There's none left.'

'And the device?'

'I threw it away.'

'I don't believe you,' said Sweeney.

'I don't care what you believe,' Jana said, snarling again as the wolf rose even more. 'Let Ceri go and get off my territory.'

Sweeney spared her a cool glance. 'I expected better from you, Jana. You could have a bright future with Segolia.' She turned to her men. 'Bring the boy. We're leaving.'

Tom backed away as Jana and Ceri leapt to stand in front of him, wolf teeth fully on display. Shannon reached out blindly and grabbed a weapon from the kitchen counter, only belatedly realising that she'd picked up some plastic salad tongs. Still, it was better than nothing. She stood in front of Tom with Ceri and Jana, facing off against Sweeney and her men.

There was a sudden movement at the window. Victoria Sweeney, yellow-eyed and fangs bared, whipped her head around.

It was Mr Jeffries. He was still in his crash helmet, staring at them all in horror. There was a second of absolute stillness as everyone realised what had happened. Then Jeffries turned and ran, stumbling away from the window, absolutely petrified.

Sweeney and her men charged after him, snarling.

Twenty-three

Jeffries ran for his bike. He pedalled away as fast as he could, but the men with yellow eyes appeared right beside him as he turned a corner. Yelling in fright, he jumped off and fled into the forest, dodging trees and running deeper and deeper in until he found a trunk to hide behind. He stopped, catching his breath, listening. He couldn't hear anything except the wind in the branches over his head and the birds, singing. Had they given up? Had he lost them?

He stepped out of his hiding place and looked around. Nothing. No twigs snapping underfoot, no distant shouting . . .

Jeffries turned in a circle. Nothing.

Then, there she was – the tall woman with fangs. She came out of nowhere, like a phantom. One minute the forest was empty, the next she was in his face. Then her men were there too, holding him still.

The woman advanced on him, her teeth bared, but her way was blocked by Jana and Ceri. They stepped between Jeffries and Sweeney, their teeth also showing, and snarling.

'Jana,' Jeffries said, 'go back to the house and call the police.'

'She won't do that,' Sweeney said, in a strangely soft voice, looking at Jana. 'Will you?'

'You can't do this!' Jana shouted. 'He won't cause any harm.'

'He saw who we are,' Sweeney said, moving forward slowly. 'The secret is paramount. You know that. It's the law. *Our law.*'

Something surged out of the trees, knocking the two security men flat and freeing Jeffries in the process. The teacher turned to see a huge grey wolf standing over the men, its muzzle drawn back in a snarl that showed all of its extremely sharp teeth. The creature moved to stand in front of him, between Jana and Ceri. Then, suddenly, the wolf was gone, replaced by someone Jeffries recognised only too well.

Rhydian Morris.

'My territory,' Rhydian said to Sweeney, his voice low and dangerous. 'My law. You let him be.'

There was the sound of someone running, crashing through the undergrowth, and Tom and Shannon arrived, joining the group that surrounded Jeffries.

'Fine,' Sweeney said, eventually. 'Deal with it. But if the truth gets out, I won't be responsible for the consequences.'

She and her men slunk away into the forest, as silently as if they had never been there in the first place.

'Um,' Shannon said, breaking the silence with an awkward smile at Jeffries. 'How about a cup of tea, sir? Come on,' she added, taking his arm. 'It's all right . . .'

They all trooped back to the house, quiet with the shock of everything that had happened and what it could mean. Shannon sat Jeffries down at the kitchen table while Ceri made him tea. Then they all sat around looking at each other for a while, as if no one could quite work out what to say. They were waiting for Jeffries to break the silence.

'So Liam was right,' he said, finally. 'Werewolves!'

Rhydian flinched at the term. 'Wolfbloods,' he corrected. 'We're what werewolves are based on, I suppose. But we're not animals. We can control our wolf-selves . . . Most of the time.'

Jeffries cast his gaze around the room. 'All of you – all Wolfbloods.'

'Er – actually Tom and I aren't,' Shannon told him.

Jeffries looked over at Tom. 'But I saw your eyes . . .'

'Yeah,' said Tom, thinking it best not to explain that one right now. 'It's . . . kind of a long story . . .'

Rhydian tried to pull the teacher's attention back to the more pressing issue at hand. 'Mr Jeffries,' he said.

'We're not the only ones involved. There are Wolfbloods all round the world.'

Jeffries looked at him warily. 'Is that why Maddy left? Because of Doctor Whitewood's allegations?' At Rhydian's nod, he went on, 'And Liam's theories, the treasure of the ancient wolf tribe, all those odd people claiming to be part of . . . of your family?' He looked at Jana. 'How could you not tell me?' Jeffries turned to Shannon and Tom. 'What if they transformed in school and hurt someone?'

'They're not monsters, sir, OK?' said Tom. 'They're pupils – like us.'

'They won't hurt anyone,' said Shannon. 'Rhydian and Jana deserve the same chance as everyone else.'

Jeffries got up. 'I'm going home. I need to think about this.'

'Sir?' Rhydian called after him quietly. 'You always said I could tell you anything. Now's your chance to prove it.'

Jeffries paused for just a minute. Then he walked out.

Jana let out a long breath. 'I suppose that's it, then,' she said. 'We just have to wait and see.'

Shannon squeezed her hands together. 'Either he'll keep the secret . . .'

'. . . or he won't,' Tom finished for her.

'What do we do?' Ceri asked. 'If he doesn't?

They all looked at each other. None of them knew, and that was probably the most frightening thing of all.

Next morning, Rhydian, Shannon, Jana and Tom stood together in the playground, still mulling over what had happened the night before.

'Well, I spoke to Becca last night,' Shannon said. 'She called Jeffries, but he didn't answer.'

'So is that a good or bad thing?' asked Jana.

Shannon shook her head. 'I don't know. Alex was there too. He told us not to panic. He said he'll try to help us even if things go wrong.'

Rhydian made a face. 'We can't rely on Kincaid, or anyone else. If Jeffries blabs, this is all on us . . .'

Tom looked up as the Ks went by, his eyes searching out Kay, but she purposefully avoided his gaze.

'Oh look,' said Katrina. 'It's the Incredible Sulk.'

'Mr Can't-explain-himself,' Kara added.

Tom threw up his hands. 'Is this going to go on forever?'

Kay snapped at that, turning around sharply. 'Yes, it is,' she said. 'I gave you a chance to explain – and you just walked out.'

Tom had had enough of this too. 'Fine,' he said. 'You want to know what's up with me? Ask Jeffries. See what you think of me then!'

Kay turned her back and walked off as Shannon, Rhydian and Jana looked at him as if he were mad.

'What are you doing?' Jana asked.

Tom wasn't in the mood. 'I don't know how you do this,' he said. 'Lie after lie after lie.'

'Because we don't have a choice,' Rhydian reminded him. 'You do! If Jeffries tells the Ks . . .'

'Well,' Tom pointed out, 'at least then we'll know where we stand.'

Jeffries was late and came in looking as if he hadn't slept all night. 'Settle down,' he ordered the class tiredly.

'Sir,' piped up Kara, as Jeffries tried to settle himself. 'Kay needs to ask you something. It's about Tom.'

Kay shot Kara a look that would have killed her if it had been sharper.

'About . . . Tom?' Jeffries asked uncertainly.

'It's about his behaviour, sir,' Kay said eventually. 'I mean, he hasn't been expelled, so there must be an explanation. Right? Tom said to ask you.'

Jeffries looked over at the corner where Tom sat. 'Is that true?'

Tom shrugged. 'Yes, sir. If you want to tell them . . . tell them.'

There was a moment of absolute silence. Rhydian felt the tension in his stomach like a solid ball. This could change everything, forever . . .

189

'The explanation, Kay,' Jeffries said, after another moment, 'is that I've had a letter from the hospital confirming that Tom was suffering from hypoglycemia. It caused a kind of hyperactivity.'

Rhydian, Jana and Shannon almost exploded with the relief, letting out lungfuls of air.

'Oh,' said Kay. 'Right.'

'Look,' Tom said to her, leaning over his desk. 'I'm sorry.'

Kay didn't smile, but she did nod. Apology accepted – at last.

Later, they went to see Jeffries in his office, but he just blanked them when they brought up the subject of what he'd seen.

'I'm busy,' he said shortly. 'Please go to your next class.'

Clearly Jeffries had decided to simply pretend the previous day had never happened. They backed out of the room just as Rhydian's phone rang.

The number on the screen was one he didn't recognise. 'Hello?'

'Hello, son,' said his dad's voice. 'I'm back.'

Twenty-four

Dacia Turner called just as Rhydian and Ceri were getting ready to go and meet Gerwyn.

Rhydian answered his phone and flicked on the speaker. 'Thanks for getting back to me.'

'I didn't want to call until I had something,' Dacia told him. 'The Cerberus account – I found something. I need to ask your dad some questions. Where are you meeting?'

Rhydian looked at Ceri. He didn't really want to tell anyone at Segolia something like that, even Dacia.

'Rhydian?' Dacia prompted.

'I thought you were flying to Norway for full moon?' he asked.

'Later,' Dacia told him. 'Look – do you want to clear his name, or not?'

Ceri nodded at him. 'All right,' said Rhydian. 'Have you got a pen?'

He told her where Gerwyn had said he would meet them, and hung up. Anxiety swirled in Rhydian's stomach, but he tried to push it down. So much had happened where Segolia was concerned that it was hard to tell what was instinct and what was just unfounded worry.

'Come on,' said Ceri, 'or we will be late.'

They struck out towards the statue of the eagle. Rhydian was looking forward to seeing his father again – maybe this time he would actually get a chance to spend some time with Gerwyn – but Ceri was still cautious.

'Some people don't change, Rhydian,' she said softly. 'Not even as wolves.'

'We talking about you or him?' her son asked.

Ceri sighed. 'You and Jana are my family now. Not your dad.'

Rhydian strode on ahead. 'Well, let's just see, shall we? The wolf knows who it belongs with, even if the human in us doesn't.'

But when they got there, Gerwyn was nowhere to be seen. His scent, though, lingered – he'd definitely beaten them to it.

'He was here,' Ceri said, looking around.

Rhydian's worries resurfaced anew. 'Something's off . . .' he muttered.

They both dropped to one knee and placed one hand on the ground, slipping into the never-ending stream of consciousness that bound them to all of nature. Rhydian travelled with the winds of Eolas, searching the forest in the golden half-light of his wolf's senses. He saw his father running through the trees, breathing hard as he fled, glancing behind him while he ducked and weaved. He was being chased by two men – city Wolfbloods. Segolia security!

'This way,' Ceri said, as they left Eolas. She took off, racing after Gerwyn with Rhydian at her side.

They found him in a dip, cornered by one of Victoria Sweeney's heavies.

'All right,' he was saying, holding his hands up in defeat. 'You win.'

'Not yet!' shouted Rhydian, relieved to see his dad in one piece.

Gerwyn turned and saw them, his anxiety immediately switching to swagger as he smiled broadly at Ceri and Rhydian. The security guard, yellow-eyed and heavily tattoed, turned with a frown.

'What's this?' he asked.

'This,' Gerwyn said proudly, 'is my family. Now – don't you have a plane to catch?'

A second guard appeared, the two of them beginning to circle Gerwyn, Rhydian and Ceri. Rhydian snarled, letting his wolf come to the surface as his eyes yellowed and the Wolfblood blackened his veins. Then two figures dropped into view from overhead. It took Rhydian the space of a shocked second to realise that it was Aran with Jana's father, Alric. They snarled at the security men.

'That is just typical, isn't it?' Gerwyn shouted, his cheeky high spirits back again in full force. 'You spend all morning waiting to catch a Wolfblood – then four turn up at once!'

Sweeney's men turned and ran. Ceri bounded over to pull Aran into a huge hug as Rhydian greeted Alric.

'Miss me, boy?' asked Jana's father, pressing his forehead to Rhydian's in greeting.

'Alric . . .' Rhydian smiled. 'How did you . . .?'

'Caught Aran's scent a few weeks back,' Alric explained. 'He told me about the pack. Meinir's betrayal.'

'Did you find the pack?' Ceri asked, but Aran's face creased into a distressed frown. He shook his head, his eyes shadowed with pain.

At Bradlington High, all the talk was of Liam's birthday present. He'd arrived on a moped that sounded like a bee stuck in a tin can, its front emblazoned with a bright red 'L' plate. He was immensely proud of his new wheels, not to mention his provisional driver's licence, while everyone else . . .

'Liam,' said Katrina, as Kay and Kara laughed outright. 'You're driving a bike that goes slower than my nan!'

'Ah,' Liam said, with a massive grin, 'but I've got a spare helmet! Who wants a go on the back?'

Meanwhile, on a bench around the corner, Dr Whitewood was trying to get Mr Jeffries to talk to her. He, on the other hand, wanted to be somewhere else – anywhere else, really – other than having this conversation.

'I'm not freaking out, Rebecca,' he pointed out impatiently. 'Just in case you hadn't noticed.'

'I almost wish you would,' she said. 'You can't keep this stuff bottled up.'

He sighed. 'I'm sorry for not believing you.'

Whitewood grinned. 'That werewolf impression you did . . . I shan't forget that in a hurry.'

Jeffries really wasn't in the mood for humour. Then he heard a sound coming from the playground. 'What is that noise?' He peered around, and saw Tom and Shannon standing at the corner, watching them.

'They're worried about you,' said Dr Whitewood.

'There's really no need,' Jeffries told her. He sighed again. 'All right. OK, look. I have . . . anxieties. What if Rhydian or Jana . . . I don't even know the correct verb . . .'

'I think the term is to "wolf out",' Whitewood supplied helpfully.

He shook his head in disbelief. Talking about this was

just absurd. It was all just absurd. 'I didn't ask for this responsibility,' he said.

'All they need to know is you're on their side,' said Becca.

Jeffries shook his head. 'I don't even know which way is up, never mind which side I'm on,' he pointed out. The weird sound was getting louder. 'What *is* that noise?'

Just then Liam buzzed around the corner on his moped with Jimi Chen on the back. The teacher couldn't believe it. 'What are you two doing?' he shouted, outraged. 'This is a school! Liam – keys! Now!'

Liam wasn't sure what was worse – having to give up the keys to his beloved birthday present or seeing Dr Whitewood back at Bradlington High.

He cornered Tom, Shannon and Jana later in class. Their teacher hadn't been his normal self for days – he was distracted and nervy, as if he'd had a real shock.

'What's going on with Jeffries?' he asked, leaning over Tom's desk.

Tom shrugged, making a face. 'Why ask us? It's not our fault he confiscated your bike keys.'

'I'm not talking about the bike,' Liam said impatiently. 'He hardly said a word in registration. Is something going on between him and Whitewood? Come on,' Liam insisted. 'I saw you watching them. You two know something.'

'Oh, here we go,' said Tom. 'You're not getting all Buffy the Werewolf Hunter on us again, are you?'

Liam frowned as Jana shot Tom a look. 'No,' he said. 'Why'd you say that?' Liam glanced around, and then added, 'Everyone knows he likes her.'

'Er . . . yes,' said Shannon. 'But no – I think they were just talking about science, Liam.'

Liam gave up and went back to his desk, looking back at Tom to see Jana punching him in the arm. What was that about?

Out in the forest, the Wolfbloods were on the move. Rhydian was still reeling from Dacia's betrayal.

'She must have been in Sweeney's corner all along,' he said unhappily. 'We think Sweeney's behind Cerberus – framing you for whatever she's up to.'

'I shouldn't have called you,' said Gerwyn. 'I shouldn't have come back.'

'Why did you?' Ceri asked.

'Because I wanted to spend full moon with my family.'

'Well, thanks for that,' Ceri said, with an edge of sarcasm to her words. 'Now we're all in danger. Again.'

Gerwyn sighed. 'When you're living on the streets, scavenging in bins, Segolia feels like a long, long way away . . .' He stopped. 'You know what? I'm going to go.'

'No,' Ceri told him firmly. 'We stick together. All of us. Together, we're strong.'

'This isn't my fight, Ceri,' Alric protested. 'I'm only here for Jana. She lost her pack. She needs her father. I need to make amends for disowning her.'

'Jana's involved too,' Rhydian pointed out. 'We all are.'

Aran stopped, suspicious. 'So . . . what are we doing? Where are you taking us?'

'Out on to the moors,' Rhydian told him. 'It's safer there.'

Alric stopped too. 'I'm not going anywhere until I see my daughter,' he said. 'This Sweeney doesn't scare me, and you said Jana's involved.'

'I want to see my alpha,' Aran added. 'Now.'

Rhydian and Ceri looked at each other, trying to decide what to do.

The class were back with Jeffries for a revision period when Rhydian turned up. They had been pushing to be let out early – after all, what was the point of staying in school to revise when they could be at home doing the same thing? Jeffries was having none of it. So, when Rhydian walked in, large as life and asking to see Jana, Tom and Shannon, it didn't go down too well when Jeffries let them all walk out, just like that.

'Sir!' Kara protested, while Katrina shook her head in disbelief.

Liam stood up. 'You confiscate my bike keys and they get to do whatever they want. How is that fair?' He shook his head, looking at Jeffries in disgust. 'You're supposed to be their teacher, sir!

Jeffries' head snapped up at that, and the class didn't think they'd ever seen him quite as angry as he was with Liam just then. 'Get out!' he shouted. 'Take your books and stand in the corridor. Go on. And you can stay behind with me in detention tonight!'

The class fell silent as Liam gathered his things and left the room.

Down the corridor, Rhydian was filling the rest of them in on what had happened that morning. Jana could hardly believe it.

'My dad's there too?' she asked.

Rhydian nodded. 'And he wants to see you. To make amends.'

Shannon was sceptical. 'Are you sure you believe him? Last time he tricked her then said she was dead to him.'

'He's not that man any more, I can sense it,' said Rhydian. 'Look, we don't have time to talk about this – my dad's in danger.'

'What if Sweeney's mob shows up again?' Tom asked.

Shannon got her phone out of her pocket. 'I'll call Alex. We can trust him.'

'I thought I could trust Dacia,' Rhydian pointed out.

'He's already helped Tom,' said Shannon. 'What did Dacia do? Nothing.'

Rhydian nodded. It was true, and they needed all the help they could get.

'You know what happens when you corner a rat,' Alex told Shannon, once she'd got him on the line and explained what had happened. 'It attacks. She feels threatened. I'm gathering evidence Sweeney's behind Cerberus. I'm taking it to the board. There are files dating back years. Things Gerwyn could help with . . . Is Rhydian there?'

Shannon handed Rhydian the phone, relieved. At least they had one person on their side that they could rely on . . .

'Listen,' Kincaid said to Rhydian. 'You and your friends can't stay anywhere near Stoneybridge tonight. Sweeney has got humans on her team. Marksmen with tranquilliser guns. You wouldn't stand a chance.'

Rhydian rubbed a hand over his face. 'What are we supposed to do?'

'I've got a place,' Kincaid said. 'It's way off Sweeney's radar. You can wolf out safely there. Where shall I pick you up?'

Rhydian thought for a moment, and then said, 'There's a landmark – an old Celtic cross, in the forest. It's on the map.'

'OK,' said Kincaid. 'I'll be as quick as I can. Turn your mobiles off. She'll be monitoring calls in that area.'

None of them had any idea that Liam had crept up to the darkroom door and listened to everything that had been said.

Twenty-five

Shannon insisted on hanging around at school even after the last bell had rung. 'I don't like the idea of Liam in detention, alone with Jeffries,' she explained, as she and Tom crept back up the corridor.

But Liam wasn't in the classroom at all. It was just Jeffries . . . and Victoria Sweeney. She was leaning over the teacher's desk in full-on threatening mode.

'Just tell me where Rhydian and Jana went,' Sweeney was saying, veining up, eyes yellow.

Tom spotted Liam at the end of the corridor. Liam jerked his head, summoning him. Shannon stayed put while Tom went to see what Liam wanted.

'There's no one coming,' Sweeney added, still looming over Jeffries. 'It's just us.'

'What will you do to them?' Jeffries asked.

'Nothing. It's Rhydian's father I want.' Sweeney sighed and took a step back, attempting to be less intimidating. 'Look, I don't mean to alarm you. And I know we didn't exactly start off on the right tack. But I am trying to protect Rhydian and Jana. His father's a criminal.'

Jeffries sighed. Outside, Shannon began to panic. He wasn't going to give them up, was he? Sweeney obviously thought so, because she smiled.

'I knew you'd understand,' she said quietly. Then she frowned as Jeffries stood up and took his phone out of his pocket. 'Who are you calling?'

'A journalist friend of mine,' Jeffries said calmly. 'I'm going to talk all about you. Because I think you're the biggest threat to these kids. I think the secret is so important to your species that you'd rather go down alone than implicate others. Or am I stating the obvious?'

Shannon breathed a sigh of relief.

Out on the stairs, though, things weren't going so well.

'Who is that woman?' Liam asked.

'What woman?' Tom asked, acting clueless.

Liam shook his head. 'I'm sick of your lies, Tom. I'm in detention, she walks in, Jeffries acts all scared and I get sent home! What's going on?'

Tom sighed, trying to find a way of throwing Liam off the scent. 'Look,' he said, at last. 'Girl Guide's honour and all that . . . Rhydian's dad got caught embezzling money from Segolia and that woman's trying to find him.'

'Then why is Jeffries so spooked about you lot?' Liam

asked, not giving up. 'Why have Rhydian and Jana gone to the old Celtic cross?'

There was a sudden movement on the stairs above them, and Dacia Turner appeared. Tom realised with a sickening jolt that she'd heard everything.

'Thanks,' she said, heading towards the classroom.

'You idiot!' Tom yelled at Liam, chasing after her. 'You don't know what you've done!'

Dacia strode into Jeffries' classroom and spoke straight to Sweeney. 'I know where they are,' she said.

'You didn't tell her?' Shannon said to Tom, horrified, as the two Wolfbloods left.

'Of course not!' Tom said, as he and Liam arrived on the scene. 'Liam gave it away.'

'Don't blame me!' said Liam, 'I haven't got a clue what's going on!' He looked at Jeffries. 'But you do. Don't you, sir?'

Tom and Shannon were already running. They couldn't call Rhydian or Jana, their phones would be off.

'Where are we going?' Tom asked, running with Shannon.

'To do the only thing we can,' Shannon shouted. 'Come on!' She ran into Jeffries' office while Tom stayed by the door, checking to see that the teacher wasn't going to follow them. Shannon searched Jeffries' desk until she found the keys to Liam's moped. 'Got them!'

They ran out towards where Liam's sad little motorbike was parked. 'Shan, this is mental – you can't drive that thing,' Tom said, as she hopped on it and then tried to work out where the key was supposed to go. 'I mean – you literally *can't* drive that thing.' He glanced over her shoulder to see Jeffries and Liam running towards them. 'Oh – great!'

'Shift,' Liam said, snatching the keys. 'Go on, get off! The old Celtic cross, right?' he said, as Shannon slid from the seat, defeated. 'I know a shortcut through my dad's land. We can get there before them.' Liam climbed on and started the engine.

'Sir?' Tom asked Jeffries, who was busy getting on his own bike.

'Sorry, I had no choice,' said the teacher. 'And I felt he deserved to know.'

'But I'll believe it when I see it,' Liam told them. 'Are you lot coming, or what?' he shouted, as he took off on the moped.

Shannon and Tom looked at each other, and then ran for their bikes.

Jana was nervous about seeing Alric again. The last time she'd seen him, he'd thrown her away from him as if she was worth less than nothing. She'd been hurt by that, not to mention angry. She wasn't sure she ever

205

wanted to forgive him – she wasn't sure a strong alpha should.

'Jana . . .' Alric began, trying to pull her into a hug, but she pushed him away.

'I'm here for them, not you.' She turned to Gerwyn. 'Help is on the way.'

'Alex Kincaid,' Rhydian explained. 'He's going meet us here. He says he can keep us safe and clear your name.'

Gerwyn looked surprised. 'Alex Kincaid wants to help me?'

'Why should we trust this man?' Alric asked.

Ceri stood between them. 'If Rhydian and Jana say we can trust him,' she said firmly, 'then we can trust him.'

Alex Kincaid arrived in a blue transit van. 'Sorry it took so long,' he said, as he jumped out and opened the back. Pulling out two cooler boxes full of chicken, he passed the first to Rhydian and another to Aran. 'Help yourselves. There's cooked *and* raw in there.'

The Wolfbloods were delighted – this close to a full moon, they were craving meat even more than usual.

'OK,' said Kincaid, as everyone munched happily. 'Let's get out of here as quickly as we can. There's no point in hanging around with Sweeney on the case.'

'Yeah, well . . .' said Gerwyn, with his mouth full.

'No offence, Alex, I appreciate the help – but I'd really love to know what is going on. We all would.'

Kincaid nodded. 'All right,' he said. 'But this is going to have to be quick. Sweeney can't be far behind us.' He perched on the back of the open van. 'Sweeney's making a bid to take control of the company. She wants city Wolfbloods to have Ansion and Eolas, and she wants humans to have Wolfblood abilities as well. She's the one behind that serum that Tom took – I identified the applicator Tom found from being from the batch that was stolen. That's what this is all about . . . She's covering her tracks. Passing on the blame to someone else.'

Rhydian looked at his dad. 'Like you.'

'Yes – exactly,' nodded Kincaid. 'You discovered the discrepancy in company accounts, so she framed you. You're all in danger now. She'll want to silence anyone who knows anything – me included. So please – can we go?'

A noise filtered down through the forest – they turned to look as a car appeared in the distance.

'It's probably her,' Kincaid shouted. 'Get in!'

'Where are we going?' Rhydian asked, as they all scrambled into the van.

'Somewhere safe,' Kincaid assured them, rushing to shut the doors as Gerwyn stayed on the ground.

'I've put you in harm's way too long,' he said, to Ceri and Rhydian. 'I'm sorry.' He slammed shut the door. 'Sweeney must never know you're helping me,' Gerwyn told Kincaid. 'Go! Go on – go!'

Kincaid ran for the driver's seat, taking off along the track at high speed. Gerwyn watched it go, feeling oddly light-headed. The approaching car speeded up before skidding to a halt in front of him. Sweeney and her men leapt out of it with Dacia Turner behind them.

Sweeney looked at the van, so far away already. 'Who's your accomplice, Gerwyn?' she demanded. 'Who's driving the van?'

Gerwyn yawned, suddenly overcome with a desperate tiredness. 'I don't have an accomplice,' he said. 'He was just some guy asking directions . . .'

Sweeney growled in annoyance and grabbed at Gerwyn, shoving him into the back of the car and slamming the door.

'What now?' Dacia asked.

'We stop that van,' Sweeney snarled, getting back into the car.

But before they could pull away, something sped out of the trees to block the road. Liam flipped up the visor on his helmet as Jeffries, Tom and Shannon all arrived on their bikes, dumping them right in front of the car.

Victoria Sweeney got out, skin veining with Wolfblood rage, eyes yellowing as she yelled at them all. 'Get out of the road!' She turned on Jeffries. 'Are all teachers this mature, or just you?'

Jeffries smiled grimly. 'Just me.'

Behind them, Tom crept to the back of Sweeney's car. They couldn't hold them up forever with a couple of insubstantial road blocks, but if he let one of the tyres down it might just give Kincaid a head start . . .

'I don't understand you,' said Dacia to Shannon. 'Why do all this for a man who stole? Committed a crime?'

Shannon shook her head in disgust. 'You don't know, do you? What Cerberus really is? How your boss here is behind it all?'

'Excuse me?' said Sweeney. 'You think I'm behind Cerberus? Who told you that rubbish?'

'You won't trick me into betraying my friends,' Shannon went on hotly. 'Who was the man you took prisoner? Someone else who found out the truth?'

'And where is he now?' Tom added, rejoining the group.

Sweeney shrugged. 'Ask your mentor Alex Kincaid. He lost him.'

Shannon blinked, confused. 'Alex Kincaid?'

'The man escaped from his lab,' said Sweeney.

'I – I don't understand,' Shannon said. 'Alex was helping you?'

Sweeney nodded. 'Was – and is.'

Dacia stepped forward, speaking up. 'Shannon. You've got it all wrong. Gerwyn's file was based on evidence provided by Alex.'

'He's the one who gave me Gerwyn in the first place,' Sweeney added. 'I didn't make anything up.'

'You're lying,' said Shannon, in disbelief. 'Alex wouldn't do that. He's been helping us.'

Sweeney stared at her. 'Helping *you*?' A sudden realisation flickered across her face. She strode past Shannon to the car, pulling open the back door. Inside, Gerwyn was passed out – completely unconscious. Sweeney growled. 'We've got to get after that van. *Now!*'

Then she looked down and saw her rear tyre. It was completely flat.

'Sorry . . .' winced Tom.

The van rocked and wobbled as it sped up the driveway towards an old stately home. A man and a woman stood on the gravel outside, silently waiting for Kincaid to arrive. He smiled as he got out, pulling open the back doors with a flourish. Inside, the Wolfbloods languished, sleeping – drugged, thanks to the meat he'd given them. *Greedy creatures,* he thought. *I knew it would work.*

He turned to the woman standing behind him.

Meinir looked in, eyes wide as she recognised her pack.

Twenty-six

Rhydian kept seeing flashes – of people, of places – but he couldn't work out if he was dreaming, or awake. Where was he? Was that . . . Meinir? No, it couldn't be. What was this place? A dungeon? There were bars . . . He had to try to keep his eyes open. He had to try to wake up . . . Had to . . .

Darkness rose up around him again. He slept.

The next time he woke, there were flames. He jerked upright, his wolfish fear of fire trumping the fogginess in his head. Rhydian looked around, eyes still bleary. He was in a cell – no, correction, *they* were in a cell. Jana and Ceri were here with him, still unconscious. So were Aran and Alric. But . . . there'd been others, too. Weren't there? Or was he still dreaming?

'Jana,' he called, shaking her. '*Jana!*'

Jana came around, blinking and struggling to clear her head. She got to her feet, standing beside Rhydian. They watched as the shapes in the shadows solidified into people.

'My pack!' Jana whispered.

But these weren't the wild Wolfbloods they knew – they were quiet and subdued. There was no fight in them, no . . . no *wolf*.

Aran got to his feet, stalking towards the pack. 'Where's my sister?' he asked. 'Where is Meinir?'

A noise echoed behind them – footsteps, coming closer. The place really was a dungeon – the bars that formed the cells were old and rusty, the stones underfoot uneven, like cobbles. It looked medieval, Rhydian thought. Like something from the Dark Ages . . .

All such thoughts fled as Kincaid came into view. He was pulling a woman – *Meinir!* – along by the arm, holding a burning torch in the other. The wild Wolfbloods recoiled from the flames, but Meinir seemed less afraid of the fire than she was of Kincaid and the Wolfbloods themselves.

Something was wrong. Meinir *smelled* wrong.

'Meinir?' Jana whispered.

'What – what are you?' Aran asked, staring at his sister.

But it was Kincaid who answered. 'She's human,' he said, with a satisfied smile. 'Free of her primitive fear of fire. Free of the animal curse you all have to live with. Welcome to Cerberus – the end of Wolfbloods.'

'You can't make a Wolfblood human,' said Ceri, as Kincaid forced Meinir to take the flaming torch and then unlocked the door. 'It isn't possible.'

213

Kincaid pushed Meinir into the cell. 'Science makes anything possible.' He shut the door again, locking it.

'Why would Sweeney help you do this?' Rhydian asked, trying to make sense of it all. 'What's in it for her?'

Kincaid uttered a short laugh. 'Victoria Sweeney? Help me? You are joking?'

'Isn't this Segolia?' Rhydian asked, confused.

'No,' said Kincaid. 'But someone had to pay for my research.'

Rhydian stared at him, the truth hitting him squarely in the face. 'So it was you who took that money, and framed my dad. It wasn't Victoria. It was you.'

Kincaid smiled, but said nothing. He didn't need to.

'Why my sister?' Aran asked, still staring at Meinir. She held out the torch, terrified, keeping her former pack – her family – at bay.

'Because she fought back,' said Kincaid. 'No fight in her now, though, is there?'

'You can't do this!' Ceri cried. 'You're a healer!'

'And I'm curing you,' Kincaid said. 'Curing you from your pain. Your anger, your hurt, your predatory nature. Your wolf.'

Alric snarled. 'Come in here and cure us. Let's see what happens.'

'Already done,' Kincaid said, with a finality that made Rhydian's blood run cold. 'You, while you were unconscious. Your pack, days ago. Full moon normally triggers your transformation – but tonight, in just over an hour, you won't become wolf – you'll become human. And you'll stay like that forever.'

He walked away, leaving the Wolfbloods in stunned silence and Meinir crying quietly.

'Meinir,' Jana said, when Kincaid had gone. 'What happened? Why are you even here?'

Meinir stared at her, afraid. There was loneliness in her eyes too, Jana realised. A deep, awful loneliness. 'Kincaid came with meat for the pack. Said it came from you. But when we ate, we slept, and then we were in this cage. Then, last full moon he fired a beam of light at me and . . . I didn't transform.'

'You can put that down,' Jana said gently, pointing at the torch. 'You're among your own kind, now.'

'I'm not one of you,' Meinir cried. 'I'm unnatural now. I'm a monster!'

'No you're not. You're still you. You're still strong and brave and powerful. And, human or Wolfblood, you will always be. Put that down. You've nothing to fear.'

Meinir stared at her alpha for another moment. Then, shaking, she dropped the torch outside the bars.

'We need to get out of here,' Jana told her. 'Kincaid trusts you . . .'

'No,' Meinir sobbed, shaking her head. 'We can't act against him. He has the cubs – Cadwr and Gwyn.'

Jana's heart sank.

'I might have been wrong about Victoria,' Shannon said, watching Sweeney. Segolia's chief checked on Gerwyn and then went to talk to Dacia, who had a laptop open on the bonnet of their car. She was searching Segolia's files for all information they could gather about Kincaid. Shannon sighed, feeling awful. 'It looks like it was Alex Kincaid all along.'

She and Tom had been trying to bring Liam and Mr Jeffries up to speed, but it was a lot to take in at such short notice. Especially when one of the people listening was an idiot like Liam.

'What does he want with werewolves?' Liam asked.

'Wolfbloods!' Shannon corrected him, impatiently. 'Liam, why are you even here? Sir – can't you send him home?'

'No way,' Liam said. 'You lot lied to me for two years. So whatever happens here, I want to be a part of it.'

'Whoa,' said Jeffries, 'Calm down, you two . . .'

Shannon couldn't deal with this. She went over to Victoria and Dacia. 'Where are your security guys?'

'It's full moon,' Victoria pointed out. 'They're on a plane to Norway, along with most of the board. It's just us.' Sweeney looked up as the sound of a car engine echoed through the forest. 'At last,' she said, as Whitewood pulled up.

There was barely any time to fill Becca in on what was going on before Sweeney started interrogating her, veins black and eyes yellow.

'Where's he taken them?' she demanded, grabbing Whitewood by the collar.

'I don't know,' said the scientist. 'I promise. I don't know where Alex is or what he's doing – I swear!'

Sweeney let her go, sensing that Whitewood was telling the truth.

'He must have taken them *somewhere*,' said Shannon.

'He has a penthouse in the city,' Whitewood offered, trying to help. 'And he goes to Denham Hill a lot.'

That made Dacia prick up her ears. 'Denham Hill? He was raised near there.'

Sweeney nodded – it was a start. 'Get me anything you have on his original home address,' she told Dacia. 'And check our tunnel database.'

Alex Kincaid's family home had been alive once – full of life and activity – but now the old place echoed and most of its furniture had been hidden beneath dust sheets. What wasn't covered – a desk here, a table and chairs there – was spread with papers and scientific equipment, because this was where Kincaid had put his plan for Cerberus into action. There was a treadmill in the corner too, which Kincaid had hooked up to one of his computers. It was important to be able to test how well his serum was working, after all. Kincaid's assistant Ben was running on it now, fast and steady, as if he would never feel the need to stop. *Amazing, really,* Kincaid thought to himself. *What abilities these monsters have.*

'Don't look so sad,' he told the two Wolfblood children, Cadwr and Gwyn. They were sitting quietly on one of the old sofas. 'When you reach your first transformation, you'll turn human like the others and lead a civilised life. Then if you're trustworthy, I'll give you this serum, the one Ben's been taking. And you'll still have all the abilities your species once had.'

'But he's not Wolfblood,' Gwyn pointed out, looking at Ben, still running on the treadmill.

'Neither will you be,' Kincaid assured them.

Ben slowed and turned. 'There's a car coming,' he said. 'I can hear it.'

Hearing enhanced as well, Kincaid thought, as he sent the children back to their rooms. *I must update my notes.*

He took Ben with him as he went outside, recognising Rebecca Whitewood's car immediately. Shannon Kelly was with her. Kincaid frowned. He hadn't expected these two. 'How did you know where I was?'

'You're lucky it's us, not the Sweeney,' Shannon told him.

'She's looking for you,' Becca added. 'Why weren't you honest with me, Alex? Don't you trust me?'

'All I get from you is how much you like your new Wolfblood friends,' Kincaid pointed out.

'Friends?' Whitewood repeated, incredulous. 'They cost me my job, my academic career – everything! My only friends are you and Shannon.'

Kincaid turned to Shannon, still suspicious. 'And I suppose you've suddenly seen the light too, have you?'

Shannon raised her eyebrows. 'Suddenly? You don't know what it's been like, keeping their secret. They destroyed all my research! They've taken over my *life*. You offered me a way out when you said you'd pay for my education.'

Ben stalked up to Whitewood, sniffing her hair and skin. 'Freesia perfume,' he said, a moment later. 'You had chilli for lunch. And . . . you're *nervous*.'

Whitewood swallowed, looking at him warily. 'Are you Wolfblood?'

Ben shook his head, and Shannon looked at Kincaid. 'Is it the serum Tom took?'

'That was an early version. This one has no side-effects.'

'That's amazing!' said Shannon.

Kincaid smiled. As always, Shannon's enthusiasm was infectious. 'You haven't seen the best part yet,' he said. 'Come on . . .'

He took them into the living room, straight to the computer that had shown him how well Cerberus could work. Bringing up the core file, Kincaid pointed, proud to be showing fellow scientific minds the genius of his discovery.

'A simple methylation of two genes, and Wolfblood DNA expresses as human. Tonight is just the start,' Kincaid told them triumphantly. 'Then I send the serum to my human allies in Segolia around the world. And soon the Wolfblood threat will be over.'

Twenty-seven

Huddled in their cell, the Wolfbloods were quiet.

'The moon is coming,' Ceri whispered, looking at her hands. There were no tell-tale signs of veining. 'I do not feel anything.'

Aran looked at Jana and Ceri, angry. 'This is all your doing,' he said. 'You told us we could trust humans.'

'Don't blame them,' Rhydian said. 'This is my fault.'

A sound came from behind them, the scrape of stone against stone. They all leapt up, turning to see one of the walls slowly grinding open. A flashlight appeared, then a face.

'Someone order a way out?' said Tom, appearing with a grin as they all heaved a sigh of relief. 'Come on – quick!'

Tom led them out through the ancient tunnel that Dacia had located – it looked as if it hadn't been used for decades, but the roof was still solid. It led out into the grounds of the house, where Gerwyn was waiting, along with Dacia – and Victoria Sweeney.

'Looks as if I was wrong about you,' Rhydian told her.

221

'Kincaid injected us with his serum,' he added. 'If we don't find a cure before moonrise, we become human. Forever.'

'Look,' Tom told Rhydian, 'Shan's still inside with Whitewood, OK? They were our decoys. We need to get them out.'

'I'm on it,' Sweeney said, immediately striding towards the house.

Tom, Jana, Rhydian and Alric watched from the bushes as Victoria Sweeney stood on the driveway and shouted for Kincaid. He appeared in the doorway with something in his hand that glinted red in the rising moonlight – one of his serum delivery devices. It was loaded.

'It's over, Kincaid,' Sweeney yelled, standing her ground.

'Over for you,' Kincaid told her. With that he lifted his hand to his chest, injecting himself with the red serum. Strength surged through him and he leapt towards her.

Sweeney turned and ran.

'It worked!' hissed Jana, 'Go!'

They ran into the house and found themselves in a long corridor. Ben appeared at one end of it, snarling as he ran towards them. Jana and Rhydian braced themselves for a fight, but then Ben tripped. He sprawled hard across the floor and Cadwr and Gwyn appeared from the shadows, grinning as they held up the wire they had stretched over Ben's path. They still knew a Wolfblood trick or two.

'Cadwr – Gwyn!' Jana said, hugging them close as Whitewood and Shannon appeared.

'Quick,' Rhydian told them 'we've got to find the antidote!'

Kincaid chased Victoria Sweeney down with a speed that was more Wolfblood than human. He cornered her on a dark tree-lined path, cutting off her escape.

'I'm just as powerful as you are now, Sweeney,' Kincaid declared.

Victoria snarled, her eyes and veins showing the wolf. 'I don't think so,' she said, grabbing Kincaid by the throat and smashing him back against a tree.

Kincaid merely smiled. 'Vanity always was your weak point,' he whispered in her ear. He pressed another syringe into her side and activated it, shooting a stream of green serum into her skin.

Sweeney let go of him and stumbled backwards. Kincaid reached for her, lifting her up and slamming her down so that her leg twisted painfully. She struggled up, limping now.

'Soon you'll be just like all the rest,' Kincaid told her, dragging her back to the house. She was no threat now. After all, she was only human.

He found his home being ransacked. Kincaid wasn't particularly surprised that Rebecca and Shannon had turned out to be traitors after all. There were always weak individuals who tried to stand in the way of progress.

'I don't understand it,' Shannon said desperately, completely unaware that he was watching. 'There must be an antidote somewhere . . .'

'There is no antidote,' Kincaid said calmly, gratified when they all spun around. He saw the little girl, Gwyn, standing nearby and shoved Sweeney away from him so he could grab her. 'So you escaped,' he said to the shocked room. 'It doesn't matter. You only have minutes. You're done for – and it's all down to her.' He pointed at Shannon. 'Without that pizza, I would never have perfected my serums.'

'You said you were curing diseases!' Shannon shouted, in tears.

'You're the one responsible for this,' said Tom angrily. 'Not Shannon.'

'And if we're going down,' Rhydian added, 'you're coming down with us.'

Kincaid laughed, backing out of the room with Gwyn and slamming it shut. The key turned, locking them in. Rhydian glanced at Alric and together they slammed their weight against it until it shattered, wood splintering as the planks came apart.

'Carry on searching, all of you!' Rhydian shouted, as he chased Kincaid.

They scanned the room. The place was a mess.

'This is impossible!' Shannon shouted, almost sobbing. 'We've only got a few minutes!'

'Shan . . .' Tom said, thinking.

Shannon waved helplessly at the equations scrawled on Kincaid's whiteboard. 'I don't understand this . . .'

'Shan,' Tom tried again.

'I don't even know what it means!' Shannon cried.

'SHAN!' Tom yelled. Everyone looked at him. He raised the vial of red serum. 'The serum I took. It gives humans Wolfblood abilities, right? So,' he looked at Alric and Jana, 'what if it reversed what he gave you?'

Shannon and Whitewood looked at each other. It was possible. Yes, it was possible . . .

'It . . . it won't take effect until the moon rises,' Shannon said. 'There will be no second chances . . .'

Jana and Alric looked at each other. What other choice did they have? If they did nothing at all, they were doomed to be human for sure. Alric nodded, the decision made.

'We're going to need a whole lot more than just this,' Tom said, indicating the tiny vial.

'I know where there's some,' piped up Cadwr. He took them to a secret chamber in the wall, struggling to open it with his small fingers. Inside were rows and rows of test tubes, some full of green serum – but just as many full of the red.

225

Shannon, Tom and Rebecca grabbed the red vials, fitting them into applicators and injecting their Wolfblood friends. It took precious seconds before anything happened. But then there they were – the tell-tale black tendrils of Wolfblood in their veins, the yellow shine to their eyes. It was working!

'Go!' shouted Victoria, grabbing handfuls of vials and applicators as she, Jana and Alric raced to treat the entire pack before the moon had fully risen.

Tom couldn't believe that he'd been the one to save their friends. 'I'm a genius!' he shouted.

Shannon grinned up at him. 'Yes,' she said. 'You are.' Then, before either of them knew what she was doing, she pulled him down into a kiss. Tom was so surprised that he almost forgot to kiss back.

Rhydian had Kincaid cornered, but the scientist wouldn't let go of Gwyn. The moon was rising – Rhydian could see it through the window – and he hadn't changed. He didn't even feel as if he could. It was over.

'I don't know why you hate us so much, Kincaid,' Rhydian said tiredly. 'Come on – let the child go. You've won.'

'Yeah, I have, haven't I?' Kincaid said, smiling. 'You see, you're not the only foster child who ended up with the wrong species. My foster parents were Wolfblood, like you. They had a real son. His parents thought having a human child in the house would civilise him, but it didn't. Every full moon he'd lock them in the cellar. Then he'd come up here to torment me.'

Rhydian tried to creep forward, but Kincaid still had hold of Gwyn.

'Then one full moon he transformed,' Kincaid went on. 'Almost tore my leg off – I was lucky to survive. Our parents said that he had the marwol in him, but he'd always been like that.' Kincaid's lip curled in disgust. 'Under the skin, you're all monsters.'

'Alex,' said Rhydian. 'What your brother did was wrong. But this is wrong too.'

Kincaid smiled, still clinging to the cub as he glanced out of the window beside him. Outside, the moon was full and fat. 'Sob story's over,' he said. 'You're out of time, wolf-boy.'

Outside, the others were rushing to inject the whole pack with the red serum before the moon reached its zenith. It was working – as soon as the serum flooded their veins, the Wolfbloods began to transform, eyes yellowing and teeth becoming fangs.

All, that was, except Meinir. Aran injected her himself, but she did not change. Her eyes remained entirely human, her teeth small and blunt. She sobbed as she realised what had happened.

227

'It's not working,' she said, desolate. 'It's too late for me . . .'

Aran pulled her into a hug, wrapping his arms around her. 'You're still my sister,' he told her, but that just made her weep harder.

Mr Jeffries ran up, holding one last full dose of red serum. 'That's everyone,' he said, breathless.

Ceri looked around, realising something. 'Where's Rhydian?' she asked.

'Oh no!' Jana cried, grabbing the device from Jeffries and starting to run. 'No, no, no, no . . .'

The moon was high – almost as high as it could possibly be. Jana could feel herself transforming as she burst into the house and sniffed, tracking Rhydian up the stairs and following at wolf speed. There had to be time . . . there just had to be – she couldn't lose Rhydian to the human world, not now, not forever.

She burst into the room, skidding to a halt as Rhydian turned towards her. She pressed the button on the applicator, firing the serum straight into his chest.

'No!' shouted Kincaid. '*No!*'

Jana felt herself transform completely, the full joy of her wolf self fizzing in her veins as Rhydian changed too. Together they faced Kincaid, who in his terror let Gwyn twist free of his grip. Opening the window, the scientist leapt out, dropping and rolling to safety as wolf-Jana and wolf-Rhydian leapt after him, determined not to let him escape.

Kincaid, with nowhere else safe to go, clawed his way up an old oak tree as Rhydian and Jana paced at the bottom. Rhydian howled, his call answered by the rest of the wolves who – all except Meinir – were now fully transformed. They bounded towards the tree, trapping a terrified Kincaid with no way of escape.

Tom wrapped his arms around Shannon, holding her close. It felt right. More right than anything else had in a long time, if he was honest. They watched their friends, the Wolfbloods, in their true wolf state.

Life, Tom thought to himself, *can be pretty amazing sometimes.*

Twenty-eight

Life was changing. Exams were finished and so was school – for good. Everyone was moving on. Katrina was opening a whole chain of Kafes. Kay had been accepted on to a fashion design course. Kara had got into sixth form college. Even Sam and Liam had plans – they were going to open a paint-balling centre on Liam's dad's farm. They were trying to persuade Jimi to join them in the venture.

Yes, life was changing for everyone. Including Rhydian.

The friends had gathered in the Kafe to hear the news. They were all sitting around a table – Rhydian, Shannon, Tom, Jana and Ceri. Mrs Vaughan was there with Ollie and Joe. Even Jeffries and Liam were looking on.

'This is amazing,' said Mrs Vaughan, looking at the piece of paper. 'You've even got citizenship! Funny how coincidence works, isn't it?' she added. 'I mean, first Maddy and her family move to Canada and suddenly you have a long-lost uncle in the same place . . .'

230

'Maybe it's just fate,' said Rhydian, although most of the people seated at the table knew it was anything but. Segolia had come through in the end – finally.

Jana couldn't deal with any of this at all. She got up and left the Kafe before her tears could embarrass her. Rhydian followed and they stood under the arch of Stoneybridge's little square, both thinking about how things were never going to be the same again.

'Jana? Come here,' Rhydian said, pulling her into his arms as she let the tears fall.

'You would have made a brilliant alpha,' Jana said as she pulled away and wiped her face.

Rhydian grinned and shrugged. 'Maybe I still will.'

Jana tried to smile. 'Just . . . not mine,' she said, wondering if he'd understand exactly what she was trying to say. Sometimes she wished she'd met him first, you see. Before he'd met Maddy Smith. Because then he wouldn't be going to Canada, would he? He'd be staying here – with her.

Rhydian looked at her with a fond smile. He did know. He really did.

Saying goodbye the next morning was one of the hardest things Rhydian had ever done. He'd only been in Stoneybridge for three years, but it had become home. Here he'd found his family – his mum, his dad. His pack.

Dacia waited by the car while he hugged Ceri and Gerwyn.

'So this is what happens when I come to find you,' said his dad, with a faint grin. 'You run off!'

Rhydian grinned back. 'You got the best deal,' he pointed out. 'You got Mum. Look after her, all right? Properly, this time.'

Gerwyn nodded and Ceri pulled him into a hug of her own. 'Be happy,' she told her son.

'You too, Mum,' said Rhydian, holding her close.

They parted and Rhydian took a deep breath, turning to Jana, Shannon and Tom. Tom had his arm around Shannon, his cheek against her hair. It had taken some getting used to at first, seeing his two best mates as a couple, but now it made Rhydian smile. They seemed to fit. Just like he and Maddy did.

The four of them gathered each other into a group hug. 'I'm really going to miss you guys,' Rhydian said, feeling his eyes fill with tears. 'It won't be forever, OK? Whatever we do, wherever we go – we'll *always* be a pack.'

'Love you,' Tom mumbled, as they all hugged again.

'Love you too, man.'

'Make sure you send our love to Maddy,' said Shannon.

'You know I will,' Rhydian promised.

They let each other go, and Rhydian took one last look at them all before getting into the car.

He wasn't ashamed of the tears that ran down his cheeks as they drove away from Stoneybridge. Rhydian thought that perhaps, Wolfbloods were blessed with two hearts in the same way that they were blessed with two bodies. If that were the case, he was happy to leave one behind, here with his friends.

The other he would take with him to Canada, to be where it – and he – belonged.

With Maddy.

Thank you for choosing a Piccadilly Press book.

If you would like to know more about our authors, our books or if you'd just like to know what we're up to, you can find us online.

www.piccadillypress.co.uk

You can also find us on:

We hope to see you soon!